LANDSCAPE
OF
SHADOWS

Also by Kevin Doherty

Patriots
Villa Normandie
Charlie's War
The Leonardo Gulag

LANDSCAPE
OF
SHADOWS

A NOVEL

KEVIN DOHERTY

OCEANVIEW PUBLISHING
SARASOTA, FLORIDA

ISBN 978-1-60809-585-8

Published in the United States of America by Oceanview Publishing

Sarasota, Florida

www.oceanviewpub.com

10 9 8 7 6 5 4 3 2

For Gaby, Charis and Vicky, with love

ACKNOWLEDGMENTS

My thanks go to Pat Gussin and the team at Oceanview Publishing, to my agent, Leslie Gardner of Artellus, and above all to Roz, without whom none of my novels would ever happen.

LANDSCAPE
OF
SHADOWS

PROLOGUE

THE HÔTEL PICARDIE stands on a gentle rise of land a few kilo-meters outside the small town of Dinon-sur-Authie. It is a crumbling confection of slate-roofed turrets and tall chimney stacks, and, inside, forgotten rooms and staircases that end in blank walls, the result of changes to its innards that have been made over the centuries. The east wing has been closed off, the once-graceful lawns and walled formal gardens are neglected, the ornamental maze is overgrown, the moat silted, and the only guests in these days of German occupation—if "guests" is the word for them—are Major Egon Wolff, Feldkommandant of the Dinon region, and his aide, who have taken up long-term residence, and other servants of the German Reich whose duties bring them to Dinon from time to time.

Long before the Picardie became a hotel it was the ancestral seat of the Ducs de Dinon. The last of the line was Henri, whose life-size portrait still holds pride of place beside the great stone fireplace in the main lobby. Here he stands in his powdered wig and silver-buckled high-heeled shoes, as arrogant as any pre-Revolution nobleman could be.

Henri made the mistake of being unpopular, so when times changed, he was dragged from his bed by his peasants and packed off to Paris for a rendezvous with Madame la Guillotine. Legend has it that when his severed head—no powdered wig that morning—was plucked from the basket and raised aloft for the crowd, the eyes blinked and swiveled, perhaps in search of the rest of him. The mouth worked as if to speak but no sound emerged. The head was dumped back in the basket, the cackling tricoteuses returned to their clicking needles. And that was the end of Henri.

There are other tales. On some nights, it is said, a ghostly figure can be seen wandering through the wild grounds, lost among the twists and turns of the old maze. The forlorn figure is not Duc Henri; it is the shade of a friar, Henri's confessor, who had come to know too much and was tortured to death in a secret dungeon somewhere beneath the building. Unlike the duke, the friar is said to be audible in death, praying and weeping by turns as he drifts past.

"Foolish tales from long ago," says Max Duval, owner of the Picardie, when talk among the old-timers in the bar turns to such legends. "This is 1941, not 1789, and it's not Robespierre's Terror we have to worry about. I have neither time nor inclination to bother with ghosts and ghouls. I have enough to do to keep the Picardie from falling to bits around my ears—not to mention keeping our German guests happy. These tales, they're all nonsense. Drink up, my friends. Whose round is it?"

For Max is also mayor of the township and commune of Dinon-sur-Authie; and a mayor must be a practical man, a man of good sense.

But the curious fact is that the more Max dismisses the Picardie's foolish legends, the more doggedly do the good souls of Dinon cling to the tales of Duc Henri and his ghostly friar as though they are gospel truth.

Which suits Max just fine.

PART ONE

RESISTANCE

CHAPTER 1

ON THIS SWELTERING June night, the Picardie is in almost total darkness. A single feeble bulb illuminates the main staircase. Although the light is too dim to reach anywhere else, blackout blinds are in place on every window.

Max is standing at one of the tall windows in the lobby. He will not get to bed tonight.

All is quiet but for the occasional creak of the Picardie's timbers cooling from the heat of the day. The plumbing, to which Max is ever attentive, has been silent for a good hour and more, meaning that upstairs, on the two upper floors, Major Egon Wolff and his aide are snugly asleep in their respective rooms. Both men dined well this evening on chef Bruno's boeuf bourguignon. Max kept their wine glasses well charged.

Afterwards Bruno helped him clear the dining room.

"I'll stay here tonight if you like," offered Bruno, a great hulk of a man, his bushy moustache yellowed by cigarette smoke.

Max shook his head and crated the empty wine bottles. "No need. Go home. Nothing I can't handle on my own."

"Even if there are three of them? You said three."

"I can manage."

Now Max peels back an edge of the blackout blind just enough to allow him to watch the night outside.

Behind him Duc Henri gleams dimly in the shadows.

*   *   *

There is a little wooden mannequin that Doctor Pierre Hamelin, Dinon's elderly physician, keeps in the window of his surgery. It looks like the kind of oddity an artist might possess but, according to Pierre, is a traditional teaching aid used by Chinese physicians. Its limbs can be moved into various positions. Pierre uses it to amuse and distract his younger patients.

This morning, when Max cycled past the surgery on his way to the mairie, his customary route, he saw that the mannequin's right arm was raised and the hand positioned as if waving a friendly greeting to passers-by. The figure's coolie hat was tilted at a rakish angle. The mannequin seemed to be smiling, but that was merely one of its tricks—sometimes it smiled, sometimes it frowned, depending on the angle from which it was viewed.

At this early hour Pierre would still be out on his morning calls, so Max continued on to the mairie. It was a normal morning. He tackled the day's crop of mayoral tasks: property disputes between neighbors to resolve, council meetings to plan. Hortense, his secretary, fussed and griped in her usual way about the presence of Egon Wolff a few paces away in his Kommandantur offices on the other side of the mairie's entrance hall.

"He uses the same front door as us, Max, the same entrance hall. There's no getting away from them, these damned Germans. It demeans the mairie, having Wolff there, right next door to us. And it turns my stomach."

"Get used to it, Hortense."

Her nose was in the air, as if a foul odour had offended it. "Never, Max. Never."

A normal morning.

* * *

At lunchtime he retrieved his bicycle from the lane by the mairie. Wolff's aide, smoking a cigarette outside the side door, watched him. Max paid him no heed; there was always a German somewhere, watching.

It was by now the hottest part of the day. Dogs slept in any patches of shade they could find. The sun beat down on the almost-empty streets, where there were more Germans to be seen than ordinary Dinonnais. Some of the Germans were on patrol duty and some were just passing time. Local people had more sense than to be out in such temperatures, while the Germans had no choice if they were on duty or at leisure away from their barracks— apart from the choice they had made when they marched into France in the first place.

A young trooper was trying to make the most of the shallow strip of shade cast by the surgery building. It achieved little for him. He was turned out in full kit of helmet, boots and gaiters, his belt and webbing heavy with ammunition pack, pistol and other equipment. His Wehrmacht uniform of gray serge—feldgrau, the Germans called it; field gray—was damp with sweat, his face and neck also streaming with sweat. His rifle seemed too big for him. He looked as if he might collapse at any moment.

Max arrived just as Pierre was propping his bicycle against the wall. A stooped figure, as reassuringly white haired and wise looking as any medical man could be, the very sight of Pierre was enough to restore the feeble and ailing. He was Dinon's bulwark against illnesses and contagions, its revered healer of farming mishaps.

There was movement behind the window of the surgery, the window where the mannequin stood. Patients were waiting, which obliged Pierre and Max to conduct their business out of doors—with care, because, overheated as the trooper was, he still had ears. And Max and Pierre both knew never to assume the Germans had no French.

"This weather," puffed the doctor as he glanced at Max. "Bizarre, a heatwave. When will it end, I wonder."

He produced a handkerchief and mopped his brow, then crossed the pavement and shook Max's hand. Neither of them showed any awareness of the young German.

"You know what, Max—I've had three patients with heatstroke this morning. All in a single morning."

"Unfortunate," said Max. "When will you next see them?"

A shrug, a shake of Pierre's white head. "As soon as possible, but I can't be certain. Could be as early as tonight. As always, it depends on many factors."

"They'll need medicine."

"Oh, indeed they will. I've already let Juliette know."

This being Juliette Labarthe, pharmacist and proprietor of Dinon's pharmacy.

"Perhaps they'll need further prescriptions."

"Certainly, they will. All three of them."

"Otherwise, they're in good health?"

"Perfect health, thankfully."

They chatted for a minute longer, mostly about the exhausting weather, then Max cycled off.

So. Three. Possibly as early as that night.

* * *

At the post office, Max noted that the white-painted doorstop stone was placed on its short side. He went to the rear of the building and entered the switchboard room where Laure Rioche, the switchboard operator, reigned supreme. She missed nothing, did Widow Rioche: every telephone call made from or to Dinon passed through her switchboard—and her headset.

Max departed two minutes later. In his pocket were the pages of notes that Laure had transcribed for him in her careful handwriting.

* * *

He found Auguste Froment, a small, inky man and one who was rarely happy these days, in his publishing premises and print shop in the warehouse district, surrounded by his work. In the background loomed a massive printing press. The aroma of printing ink hung thickly in the air.

Even under German occupation the ordinary cycle of life went on. People still needed wedding invitations, cards announcing the birth of a child, requiem Mass cards, flyers for football tournaments. And then there were Wolff's endless propaganda posters, stacked here and there around the cavernous room. Strips of galley proofs for Dinon's weekly newspaper, *La Voix de Dinon*, were laid out on a long table, awaiting Kommandantur approval and no doubt teeming with Wolff's regular servings of Reich pap, for *La Voix* had been turned by him into another vehicle for Reich propaganda.

And here was one of the sources of Auguste's prevailing unhappiness. He had been the newspaper's publisher, editor, roving

reporter and photographer, all rolled into one, for as long as anyone
in Dinon could remember, free to make his own decisions on what
he reported and how he reported it. But nowadays he had no choice
but to publish what he was ordered to publish.

The warehouse district tended to have less of a German presence
than the busier and more populated parts of town, but Max had
passed a patrolling trooper as he approached the yard, so he took care.

"Your technical services will be required, Auguste."

The morose little printer brightened; he grunted his approval of
this information.

"Good, my dear Max. Delighted to hear it. How soon?"

"Any time from tonight. I'll let you know."

"As soon as that? Even better."

The trooper rounded the corner; he took a few steps into the yard,
his slow approach suggesting mild curiosity rather than a specific
purpose. He gazed into the window at the examples of Auguste's
work on display.

"How is Marie?" Max asked, referring to Auguste's wife, whose
constant claims of fragile health were another source of the printer's
unhappiness.

"Feeling very low today, Max, very low. This heat is hard on her.
But then again, she can't stand the cold either."

"Pierre says you don't pay your medical bills."

The trooper was finished with the window; he retraced his steps
and departed.

Auguste rose to Max's jibe. "Pierre's lying. Always does."

It was a familiar joust. Max persisted. "He says you don't pay on
principle because you're a communist."

"You see? More lies. Communists are good members of society.
It's the capitalist exploiters like Pierre we have to watch. You tell
him from me he's a quack and a charlatan."

Max promised to do that. Auguste's spirits seemed improved by the exchange, as Max had been hoping they would be.

"So, dear Max," concluded Auguste, a sparkle in his eyes, "any time from tonight, you say. Do we know how many?"

"Three. You have what you need?"

Auguste looked offended, as though his professional competence as well as his politics was under attack.

"Of course," he replied. "Have I ever let you down?"

Max mounted his bicycle and went on his way.

*   *   *

Later, as he returned from lunch at the Café du Commerce and passed Pierre's surgery again, he saw that the Chinese mannequin's right arm and hand, having done their work, were back in their usual place by its side. The coolie hat was straight. All was back to normal; now it was the left arm and hand that were offering their customary greeting. And the smile was still there.

CHAPTER 2

THE NIGHT IS close and airless. Dinon town is in blackout, not a single street lamp lit and every window shuttered. The waning moon, in its third quarter and only a slim crescent, is obscured by cloud, making the darkness complete.

A young woman waits restlessly in the shadows at one end of a narrow alleyway. She hates this darkness, distrusts it, this alien blackness such as never prevails in Paris, not even during its blackout, for in the city the pale stone of the buildings, the store windows, the theatre and restaurant awnings, the billboards and advertising pillars, postboxes, even road surfaces—all these catch and reflect and concentrate the slightest glimmers of light. The Seine too and its bridges, with every ripple that passes along the great river.

But nothing alleviates this darkness here in Dinon. She shudders. Yet the darkness is what she needs for the task that has brought her here.

She has never killed before. That is what she is ready to do tonight. That is why she is here. Tonight she will kill for Gérard. Tonight is for retribution. God willing, she will not fail.

She wonders what time it is. Close to midnight, certainly, but how close? The timing matters but it is too dark in these shadows to check her watch. So she waits, her eyes burning as they strain against the evil darkness.

Her task for the moment is to watch for anyone entering the alley from behind them. Up ahead is Jean-Luc. He is the one in charge. He will decide when they should make their move. He will also decide if they have to abort. She hopes that does not happen.

She is tall enough to pass for a man. As she traveled here today on the train with Jean-Luc, in separate compartments from each other, she wore a skirt and her hair was loose. Now, in the simplest of disguises, she is wearing trousers and her hair is hidden from view inside a battered black beret. If she is seen tonight, she hopes this is how she will be recalled and described—as a man.

At last, from around the corner at Jean-Luc's end of the alleyway, there is the sound of a door creaking open. A glimmer of light shows for a moment, then vanishes as the door slams shut. Male laughter drifts into the alley, accompanied by the clatter of boots on cobbles. The Germans who have emerged from the brothel stand in the street, still out of sight, laughing and talking in their unmelodic language.

There are only two voices, therefore hopefully only two men. Taking on more than two would be too risky. But it is still important to wait until they begin to move away, their backs turned, to make the most of the element of surprise. This is what she was taught in Paris.

As she moves closer to Jean-Luc she hears the scrape of a match being struck. There is a small burst of light as it flares. She smells cigarette smoke. She hears heavy footsteps. The men are on the move.

Jean-Luc steps forward, peers around the corner. He half turns towards her, his face a pale blur in the darkness, and gives a single emphatic nod. Then he is out of the alley. She follows immediately, taking up position beside him, exactly as planned, exactly as they practiced. Relief, to be in action.

One of the Germans is still laughing but the other hears the movement behind them and wheels around. His cigarette spins to the ground in a tiny explosion of sparks. Jean-Luc fires twice. She hears the ricochet as one bullet strikes the wall of the brothel but the German staggers backward with the force of the other bullet.

Then everything goes wrong.

The German is shooting as he falls—three shots, close together. He sprawls on the pavement, the gun slipping from his hand. But Jean-Luc also falls, his head smashing against the cobbles. With a sick feeling she knows that he is as dead as the German.

The other man has turned to face her. His hand descends to his holster. He draws his pistol.

She has both her hands clamped about her own weapon, is braced for the recoil, and now she squeezes the trigger.

Nothing.

No shot, no recoil.

The gun has jammed.

She wrenches at the slide of her weapon but cannot tell if it has freed itself properly. In desperation she squeezes the trigger again.

A shot rings out. It is from her pistol. The recoil jolts along her arm like an electric shock. The shot is wild, not aimed, but the German cries out. The bullet has hit him. He lurches to one side.

She can try—should try—to finish the job, which means gambling that her gun does not jam again. But the wounded German is steadying himself. His pistol sweeps upward. She knows that, unlike her weapon, his will not misfire.

And any second now the door of the brothel will burst open, disgorging God knows how many armed soldiers to investigate the shots they heard.

The German opens fire but he is too late. She has already flung herself back into the alley. She seizes her bicycle and flees.

CHAPTER 3

THE LOBBY OF the Picardie remains still and silent. Outside, nothing stirs as Max watches. No shadows shift in the overgrown grounds, the thin moon drifts behind cloud, no reflection disturbing rue de la République.

Suddenly the silence is broken. Two sharp cracks, like firecrackers, echo somewhere in the night. They are not near, but the sound is magnified by the silence that preceded them.

Nor are they firecrackers. They are gunshots.

Now there is further gunfire—a rapid sequence of several shots; a brief pause, a single shot; finally, another volley.

They are happening in Dinon.

From upstairs come sounds of frantic movement. The gunfire has woken Wolff and his aide, their windows open wide for any breath of air on this stifling night.

Max hears doors being flung open. The Germans call loudly, urgently, to each other, a floor apart. Doors slam shut, then strike walls as they are flung open again. Now there is the thud of running feet overhead—heavy, booted feet—and both men come hurtling down the stairs, fastening tunics and gun belts as they descend.

Neither man notices Max, who has retreated to the shadows. They make for the courtyard and garage block. Seconds later he hears the roar of an engine and the screech of tires as Wolff's armored car accelerates away.

*   *   *

Silence settles over the Picardie again. Max returns to his vigil at the window.

Those gunshots. Despite Wolff's seizure of all firearms held in civilian hands, despite his regular threats and edicts against illegal weapons, there will always be guns in Dinon, hidden in barns or milking parlors, stashed away under eaves, beneath floorboards, behind kitchen stoves. They are a fact of life in this community.

Guns have their different voices. The shots fired tonight were from handguns, not rifles. An illicit night-time poaching expedition would require rifles. And it would take place deep in the countryside, not in Dinon town.

So the gunfire tonight was not poachers at work.

Max searches for other explanations. He searches hard. He wants an explanation he can believe. Perhaps there was a quarrel between citizens. Serious enough as explanations go, but not the very worst. Not the explanation he would fear most. He would like to believe anything but that.

He extinguishes the light over the staircase and returns to the window. He opens it and listens. What he hears does not reassure him. In the distance, down in Dinon, many vehicles are on the move, their engines whining and revving. There is the racket of truck doors slamming, tailgates crashing open or closed. Coarse voices bellow commands. He hears the clank of machinery, then the thump of heavy equipment, a pattern of sound that is repeated and repeated as he listens. He fits images to the noises, picturing roadblocks being set in place, streets and lanes being cut off, armed troopers taking up position, their boots ringing on cobblestones.

If the gunfire was a shoot-out between citizens, it would be a matter for Dinon's irascible police chief, a stunted little individual by the name of Jacques Dompnier, and his louts. Perhaps they are already involved. The gunfire might even have been theirs—they are armed and roam Dinon and its environs at all hours of the night, theoretically under Wolff's control. Theoretically only, for Dompnier is not a man to be easily or willingly constrained. But even if his men were responsible for the gunfire, the police chief has no heavy equipment that would make the din that Max is currently hearing.

No, this is far beyond Dompnier and his gang. A major operation is being mounted. A military operation.

Which means that Egon Wolff is sealing Dinon tight, locking it shut, making it a cage that no one can enter or leave.

Now Max becomes aware of another sound. It is the rising note of a train pulling away from rest, the rhythm growing steadily faster as the locomotive gathers speed. His gaze goes to the silhouette of the high railway embankment on the other side of rue de la République. Out of sight in the deep cutting beyond it, a freight train must have been stationary and silent, freight being the only rail transport permitted during curfew on those nights when the Germans move troops, equipment and supplies. Tonight is evidently such a night.

And now the train is under way again.

Gradually the sound fades. Max closes the window. But he stays there, watching.

CHAPTER 4

SHE HAD TO get away from the town before the Germans flooded it with troops. She skidded through the warren of unlit streets and squares, hoping that no patrol would appear in her path. She listened for the sound of motor vehicles anywhere around her but all she could hear was her bicycle wheels on the cobbles and the roar of blood in her ears.

She had the map in her mind that she and Jean-Luc had been given and that both of them had memorized, testing each other like schoolchildren. She remembers how she railed against his insistence on the tedious task.

"I understand the map's importance, of course I do," she argued. "But why do I need to memorize it when you're doing so? You'll be in charge; you can do it for both of us."

How stupid she was. Now she would find out whether she had done her memorizing well enough.

She knew that the Germans were not the only danger. The terraced rows of houses she was racing past were in darkness, but their inhabitants would be waking in response to the gunfire. Unseen eyes would be watching her, noting her progress, the watchers only too happy to report which way she went.

None of them would lie to protect her, for fear their neighbors should offer a contradictory account and be believed. They would tell the Germans what they saw because this was a town that was too cozy with its German occupiers. That was what she had been told in Paris, that the Dinonnais cannot be trusted, that she could not presume their help in any way. They would not protect her but would give her up without a moment's hesitation.

She pressed on, her senses more acute than she had ever known them, listening and watching for a German patrol that would mean the end of everything.

She kept seeing Jean-Luc as he fell dead at her feet.

Gérard as well. Always she saw Gérard.

She left the streets of narrow houses and came into open countryside. And now the hated darkness enveloped her, made her its own, the impenetrable darkness of the empty countryside. Not even the tiniest gleam of light from that hidden moon broke through. Nothing challenged the black night.

She passed the abandoned woodman's hut where she and Jean-Luc had waited until it was time to enter Dinon. After she passed the hut there were no other buildings of any kind. Only the silhouettes of trees and hedges looming from that darkness and falling away as she raced past.

As far as she could tell, the map and her memory were serving her well. But the silence of the night did not last. Behind her in the distance she heard engines roaring into life, voices shouting, metallic crashing noises, all the chaotic sounds of machinery and men. The Germans were emerging from their barracks.

The road became an uphill slog—not too steep an incline but a long and wearying one—until at last she came to the embankment behind and below which ran the railway line. Here, exactly where the map promised, she found the roadside kilometer stone that marked where the train would be. And now that she was close enough, she could hear the rhythmic beat and hiss of the locomotive down in the cutting below.

She thrust the bicycle behind a clump of gorse and scrambled up the woody slope of the embankment as fast as she could. It was hard going. The slope was steep, the undergrowth dense, but her reward at the top was to see in the cutting below her the dimmed lamps of the locomotive, steam rising over it, its furnace glowing, and behind it the long dark bulk of freight wagons.

Ten minutes, no more, that was as much as the locomotive driver and the fireman, rock-solid union men, loyal and proven résistants whose judgment was not to be doubted, had said they could risk with whatever ruse they were using on their German guards. Ten minutes they reckoned they could manage; any longer than that, however, and the guards would become suspicious.

But how long had the train been waiting already?

She swooped down the cutting in long, leaping strides, following a diagonal course that took her away from the locomotive and its lamps and towards the unlit wagons at the rear. The tangled undergrowth, as tough as steel, snatched at her legs, pierced her trousers, cut into her flesh.

She was most of the way down when the train began to move off.

She wanted to scream, tell the driver to allow her a few more seconds. But how could she scream without the guards hearing?

She did scream, but only in her mind.

She continued running. Keep going, that was the imperative.

But she did not keep going. She felt a sudden wrench on her jacket as it snagged on the unyielding undergrowth. She was spun around, lost her balance, tripped and fell.

And watched helplessly as the train gathered speed and was swallowed by the night.

*   *   *

Now she tries to gather her thoughts.

She must retrieve the bicycle. She can use the night to get as far as possible from Dinon and then try to make her way back to Paris. She has cash, she can buy a rail ticket once curfew ends and passenger trains start running again. She will cycle further than the station at the town of Rue where she and Jean-Luc disembarked on their way here, much further than that, because the Germans will look for her there. Wherever she boards she can expect extra security checks, but her hope is that the Germans will be looking for a man and by then she will have changed back into her skirt and unpinned her hair.

She begins the climb back up the cutting, a longer and even steeper climb than the embankment on the other side. She knows her strength is beginning to fade.

It is now that she discovers her skirt has gone. It was folded safely in her pocket but it is not there now. She checks all her other pockets. No skirt. She begins searching for it in the undergrowth, groping at the dark ground and foliage around her. She is drenched in sweat; it streams into her eyes, stinging, blinding her.

She forces herself to be calm. In this malevolent darkness her efforts will be futile. She could spend the rest of the night searching. And the skirt might not even be here—she could have dropped it during her ride from Dinon. Or when she fell. Or any number of other possibilities.

Time is passing, too much time. She abandons the search.

She reaches the top of the slope. She collapses, face down, and allows herself a moment to catch her breath. But the noises from Dinon have become louder and more insistent. She raises herself on her elbows. And does not like what she sees.

The slip of moon has emerged from its screen of cloud. She has come a considerable distance along the embankment, the result of her diagonal descent of the cutting. She makes out on the far side of the road below her the dark presence of several buildings, the largest one a wide turreted structure that looks like a grand château or an institution of some kind.

Whatever the place is, there was no mention of it in the briefing she received in Paris and no indication of it on the map—for the simple reason that she was never meant to end up in this spot.

The buildings are in blackout, no light showing anywhere. That means nothing, of course. As with the little houses in Dinon, eyes could be watching from any of those dark windows.

But the Germans are closing on her. She must take her chances. She stumbles down the embankment, races back to the kilometer stone, finds the bicycle, and sets off again, leaving Dinon behind.

She has only just passed the dark château when the slit beams of a pair of headlights appear on the road directly ahead of her, a good distance away as yet but coming right at her. Close behind is a second pair of beams.

A German patrol. Two vehicles, possibly with more following.

She swings the bicycle around in a turn so tight that she almost comes off, and pedals back in the direction from which she has come.

Now she has choices. She can climb the embankment again and hide on the other side. But she knows she does not have the strength to make that climb again.

She can go back towards Dinon and try to reach the woodman's hut before the Germans catch up with her, and hide there. Madness.

Or she can try to conceal the bicycle and run for cover in the meadow whose dark extent stretches behind the château. That could work, provided she can recover the bicycle once the Germans have passed by.

But when she reaches the wall that encloses the cluster of dark buildings and the grounds surrounding them, it is as if the place is drawing her into its embrace. She leaves the road and passes through the open gateway.

CHAPTER 5

MAX IS STILL at the lobby window when a German armored car and an open-backed truck pass through the Picardie's archway and rattle to a halt in the courtyard. In an earlier century horse-drawn carriages would have brought the highest in the land to Duc Henri's formal balls and musical entertainments. There would have been lanterns and flambeaux to light the way, and red carpet laid to protect delicate aristocratic footwear. But tonight, the only illumination is from the suppressed beams of masked headlights; it is heavy German boots that crunch over the ground as the truck empties and a squad of troopers—farm boys from Bavaria, bank clerks from Berlin—lumber into line, awaiting orders.

The armored car is Egon Wolff's. Max goes out to meet him.

* * *

It is a year now since Wolff came to Dinon; a year since the town became his and Germany's.

On that midsummer morning Max set out from the Picardie as a soft dawn was breaking. He was alone. He walked to the crossroads at the town limits. There he waited. He wore his mayoral sash over his chest and shoulder and was dressed in his most formal black suit. Black for mourning. The last time he had worn it was for Geneviève's funeral. It was the old priest back then, Père Bastien's predecessor and a man of tradition. Black for mourning, the old priest said, and on that if nothing else Max agreed with him.

So, black for mourning on that midsummer morning as well, for there was plenty to mourn that day. France had fallen. Her war was over. Her defeat had taken only six weeks.

The fact was almost beyond belief, but fact it was. Should there be any doubt, there came the scratchy voice of Pétain on the airwaves: Pétain the old man, the hero from that earlier war with Germany. The war in which Max fought. A war that was never to be repeated.

The old man's words to the nation crushed all hope.

"We must cease hostilities," he announced. "The fighting must stop."

A few days later, in a telephone call from the Préfecture in Amiens, Max was told that he must hand his beloved Dinon to the invaders.

"It's the same everywhere, Max. Not just Dinon. Paris has been handed over, surrendered. It's been declared an open city. Don't oppose them. Cooperate. There's to be no more bloodshed."

"Bloodshed? God forbid. Cooperate? Cooperate how?"

He could almost hear the weary shrug at the other end of the line.

"Just do the best you can, Max. It's all any of us can do."

The line went dead. A soft click told him that Laure Rioche had hung up as well.

"Looks like we're on our own, Hortense."

Hortense harrumphed. "Us and Laure Rioche."

*   *   *

An hour passed as Max waited at the crossroads. The sun climbed higher; the day warmed.

At last, he detected a faint buzz in the distance and saw a shimmer of movement on the horizon, so tentative that it could have been a heat haze. But it was no mirage. Gradually it resolved into a convoy of vehicles. The buzzing became a steady drone; it grew louder and deeper as the convoy drew nearer. A cloud of dust and exhaust smoke stained the perfect sky.

All too soon an armored car and a long caravan of open-backed trucks came bumping down the road, engines roaring. They halted a few meters short of him. He felt the heat from the engines. Each truck carried a dozen armed German troopers. The trucks were interspersed by double lines of motorcycles, their riders and sidecar occupants armed with rifles slung across their shoulders.

All the vehicles were liveried in dull camouflage shades of gray and green; each was marked with the black and white German cross.

The racket by now was horrendous. Dust whirled in the air and settled on Max's black-clad shoulders. The stench of exhaust fumes was sickening. Somewhere among the vehicles, dogs were barking.

The two occupants of the armored car were the soldier behind the wheel and, beside him, the officer whose bearing and uniform insignia showed him as the one in charge.

Max judged him to be in his thirties. He was dressed not in battledress but in formal uniform, though without a cap. He had close-cropped hair, not blonde as in the stereotype that Max had been half expecting, but black. His eyes were very blue. A strong, handsome face.

Everything about him was orderly and precise. But just then he turned his head and revealed the defect that marred those handsome features. On his left cheek was a long scar: not a thin, clean cut such as a blade would make, but a shallow furrow the width of a fingertip. It ran in a straight line from his chin to his ear. Its edges were puckered, as if the flesh had melted. It could only be the track made by a bullet.

Max saw something else. There was an Iron Cross at the collar of the German's tunic. So he was no back-room warrior: he had seen combat. Max wondered how many French lives had paid for that Iron Cross.

He saw the map the German was holding. To this man, Dinon and its people were nothing but words and lines and distances marked out on a sheet of paper, merely ground to be covered, territory to be seized. Nothing of flesh and blood, not families and lives torn by the turmoil of war and defeat.

The German seemed to be in no hurry. No need, Max realized: the German was the conqueror; he had all the time in the world. He studied Max for a while, his expression revealing nothing. His gaze took in the silk sash with its stripes of blue, white and red.

Max remained very still under his scrutiny. He had come here and that was enough; the next move should not be his.

The German vaulted down from his vehicle. He moved lightly, easily. Compared with him, Max felt heavy and dulled by standing there.

Sunlight flashed on the visor of the German's cap as he picked it up from the back of the vehicle and settled it in place. He glanced back at the convoy and raised an arm. Every vehicle engine shut down obediently. Even the dogs ceased barking.

The German turned back to Max and delivered a straight-arm Nazi salute. A small puff of dust rose as the heels of his polished black jackboots clicked together.

"Heil Hitler!"

He clasped his hands behind his back—a very straight military back—and waited for whatever Max had to say.

Max tried not to stare at the scar, an instinct of courtesy that still held, even in these circumstances.

"May we speak in French?"

"But of course." Clearly pronounced, although with a strong accent, and accompanied by the shadow of a smile, as though Max's lack of German was another victory. The smile was uneven, impaired by whatever muscular damage the scar had caused.

"My name is Duval. I am mayor of Dinon-sur-Authie."

"Thank you for coming to receive me, Monsieur le Maire. I am Major Egon Wolff. I am Feldkommandant of the Dinon region."

Max took a long breath. Now came the words that he knew might stick in his throat.

"The people of Dinon accept the situation in which France finds herself." His voice was steady. "I am here to tell you that our town and commune are open to you, as our government has required of us."

There, he had said it.

Wolff nodded slowly. "On behalf of the military forces of the German Reich, I welcome your cooperation. I intend to locate my headquarters in Dinon. My men will be garrisoned here."

"I see. The people of Dinon have expressed the wish that I continue as their mayor. I would like to be able to oblige them."

The German's eyes widened in surprise. "I would not consider otherwise. I will be counting on your assistance and support in my administration of the region. You will be an important link between the Reich's governance and the civilian population. You and I must work together for the mutual benefit of those for whom we are each responsible. That is my hope."

Hope? Max took the opening.

"And my hope is for the safety of my townspeople. There are no military personnel among us. We offer no opposition to your presence. You will meet no hostility. In return I ask that you take no action of a warlike or punitive nature and that you respect our homes and property."

"You have my word. Your citizens and their property will be safe." The German paused. "And now you will remove that sash, Monsieur. No flags or other symbols of France are permitted. Only those of the German Reich. You understand, I am sure."

The command was no more than Max had been expecting, but the reality of it was still a blow. He removed the tricolor strip, folded it with care and returned it to his pocket. Then lifted his gaze and faced the German.

And so, in shame and sorrow on that idyllic midsummer morning, the bargain was made. A bargain sealed with French tears; but it meant that Dinon and its people might be safe.

CHAPTER 6

MAX CROSSES THE courtyard as a second truck enters and lurches to a halt.

"What's going on, Major? I heard gunfire."

Wolff ignores him. The second truck disgorges more troopers to line up with their comrades. An officer jumps down from the cab of the vehicle. Wolff issues a stream of instructions to him.

Only when that is done does he address Max—but not to answer his question.

"The Hôtel Picardie will be searched."

"What? Why, Major?"

"Because I say so. Everywhere is being searched. Where have you been tonight, Monsieur?"

"Here in the Picardie, of course. Why is it necessary to search my hotel? What was the gunfire? What has happened?"

Wolff issues more orders to the officer. The officer shouts commands to the troopers, who stomp off in pairs, some towards the hotel's main entrance and lobby, some into the Picardie's grounds, others in the direction of the barn and outbuildings. Large dogs accompany each group, whining and straining at their leashes.

Wolff returns his attention to Max. But still with no intention to answer his questions.

"You say you heard the gunfire."

"Of course."

"Where were you when you heard it?"

"In my private quarters. In my rooms."

It is near enough to the truth; and as much as the German needs to know.

"I reached the lobby as you were driving off."

"Did you leave the hotel after I retired for the night?"

"I certainly did not. I never leave the premises at night when there are guests. What is this—are you interrogating me?"

"You will stay with me now, Monsieur. I require you to give my men access to all parts of the hotel. You will switch on all the lights and unlock all rooms. The Picardie will be searched, whether you agree to that or not. I advise you to agree."

"Your advice is unnecessary. Search, by all means, I have no objection. I'll help in any way I can. But remember, I have responsibilities as mayor of Dinon."

Wolff is already turning away.

"Yes?" he says absently. "And so?"

"As mayor I require you to tell me what has happened in my town and what you know about the gunfire."

"Monsieur Duval—"

"I'm putting this to you as a formal request, Major. You'll be aware that it's within the terms of my remit as mayor to make such an enquiry and it's your responsibility as Feldkommandant to provide an answer."

Wolff stares at him as if he cannot believe what he is hearing. Seconds pass. A muscle flickers behind the scar on his jaw.

"Then I will tell you, Monsieur le Maire." He enunciates the formal title with sarcasm. "You are delaying me but I will tell you. One of my men has been shot dead in Dinon tonight, another has been seriously wounded. They were ambushed by an assassination squad, no doubt a Resistance unit."

Max takes in this information. He feels anger; but also a tentative sense of relief.

"Assassination squad?" he says. "That's not—"

"Yes, Monsieur—here in your town. You look as if you do not believe me."

"I find it difficult."

"This is an act of terrorism against the Reich. There were two assassins. One has been killed, the other is still at large. He may be wounded, because the surviving soldier bravely returned fire."

"I see."

"I intend to find that missing assassin. I have called out my garrison and cordoned the town and surrounding countryside. All properties within the cordon are being searched. That includes the Hôtel Picardie. You will know that these steps are within *my* remit as Feldkommandant. I trust I have now clarified matters to your satisfaction."

"And what else do you intend?"

Wolff's gaze hardens. "I have been very patient with you, Monsieur, but my patience has a limit. I will advise you what else I intend when I have decided what is necessary. For now, my priority is to find the escaped assassin. As to your remit as mayor, you have always assured me that my soldiers would face no violence from your citizens, but I warn you—"

"You can't possibly think this has anything to do with the people of Dinon. Whoever the attackers are—these assassins as you call them—I promise you they won't be from Dinon. We have no Resistance group in this town, no sympathizers. You must surely know that."

Wolff turns away, apparently having decided there is no more to be said, but then seems to change his mind. He turns back to Max.

"Understand this, Monsieur Duval. Tonight's incident will have repercussions. They will be serious. And they will be out of my hands. You should prepare yourself."

"Is that a threat, Major?"

But Wolff does not answer.

*   *   *

As the search progresses, the Feldkommandant keeps Max by his side. His men are thorough. The lobby and public areas echo with those German boots, the contents of cupboards and cabinets are turned out, every guest bedroom is scoured, wardrobes peered into. The dogs dribble saliva everywhere. Dirty hands root through clean linen in storage cupboards. The kitchen and its larders are not spared. Max is called upon to explain every dead-end staircase and bricked-up doorway in the old building. Walls are rapped with rifle butts to check for hidden voids. The oak paneling in the lobby and dining room and library receives close attention.

The lobby's portraits, particularly that of Duc Henri in his finery, raise sniggers from Wolff's farm boys until their officers silence them.

Even the Feldkommandant's own suite is searched, on his direct orders, as is his aide's room, albeit in both their cases with more consideration than is accorded the rest of the hotel.

Then it is the turn of Max's own private quarters. These consist of a bedroom and bathroom in what was once a servants' area tucked away at the end of a winding corridor on the ground floor. Wolff's gaze takes in the bed and simple furniture. Whatever he makes of the place, he keeps his thoughts to himself.

But he is unable to ignore the photographs displayed on the small bedside table. He bends to study one in which Max and Geneviève are standing side by side, their arms linked, with the Picardie and a full complement of staff in the background—uniformed waiters, gardeners, Bruno with a line of white-aproned kitchen staff.

Wolff picks up the photograph without bothering to ask Max's permission. He indicates the image of Geneviève.

"Your wife, Monsieur? I have never seen her here in the Picardie."

"My late wife," Max corrects him. He does not conceal his resentment of the German's intrusion.

Wolff inclines his head, puts the photograph down and asks nothing more. He orders his men out of the room.

*　　*　　*

A motorcycle messenger arrives and presents himself to the Feldkommandant. Heels are clicked, salutes are presented. Wolff directs the man to a quiet corner of the courtyard, where he listens to what he has to say. More clicking of heels, more salutes, and the messenger departs. Observing from the lobby, Max knows it will not be good news.

Wolff returns indoors and eyes him in silence for a moment.

"The soldier who was wounded has died."

"I regret that, Major."

"Do you? I regret it also. Unfortunately, our regrets change nothing. Two good men are dead and regrets will not bring them back. Now tell me, Monsieur—what would you do in my position? Would you grieve? Would you write sorrowful letters to the families of these two men, to the children who will never again feel their fathers' arms about them? What would you do, Monsieur?"

"I would grieve, certainly, as I am sure you will."

"I intend to do more than grieve, Monsieur. I will do what honor demands—I will hunt down the assassin. Without mercy. And without regrets."

He orders Max to open up the east wing so that it can be searched. Although that section of the hotel has been closed for months, the electricity supply is still connected. As with the main part of the hotel, Wolff orders all lights to be switched on.

Max is unprepared for what follows. He goes to the fuse box behind the concierge's desk and pulls down the master switch. As the wall sconces and chandeliers glow into life, he no longer sees the peeling wallpaper or smells dust and mold. Time is reversed. The Picardie is again as it once was, vibrant and bright. Guests throng the east lobby, the women in gowns of every color and rich fabric, the men sleek and confident. Chandeliers sparkle, conversations are lively, in several languages besides French—including German. Waiters and porters, immaculate in burgundy uniforms, bustle about their duties, refilling glasses, pushing trolleys laden with luggage. Cigar smoke drifts in aromatic clouds. There is laughter, as clear and brilliant as the ring of the crystal champagne glasses in the hands of the Picardie's guests. Excitement crackles in the air.

Excitement and no war. In this gleaming world, France has not fallen. There is no occupation. Dinon is free. There is vivid color just as there always was—no dreary expanse of Wehrmacht feldgrau smothering everything. No swastika banners, no Egon Wolff with his battle scar and Iron Cross and Nazi salutes.

"Monsieur?" a voice is saying. "Monsieur Duval?"

As suddenly as the door to the past opened, so does it close. The vision fades. The buzz of conversation dies, the crowd vanishes. The past evaporates and there is only dust. German footprints in gray dust.

"Monsieur?" the voice says again. Wolff's voice.

Max brings him into focus. The German is studying him closely.

"Is everything all right, Monsieur?"

Anger surges like vomit in Max's throat.

"Everything is fine, Major. You're tearing my hotel and home apart, you've shown no respect for my privacy, God knows what you've been doing to my town and my citizens—but everything is fine. How could it not be?"

"Be careful, Max," whispers a voice. But not Wolff's voice. This time it is Geneviève's voice that Max is hearing.

* * *

In the Picardie's grounds, powerful flashlights scan the overgrown shrub beds. Troopers fix bayonets to their rifles and trample through the old maze, plunging the bayonets into the dense hedging. All they get for their trouble is sprigs of hornbeam impaled on the blades and fouling their gun barrels.

They turn their attention to the orchard, their flashlights sweeping along the high dry-stone walls and between the rows of apple trees. The dogs race back and forth, dragging their handlers after them. The grass beneath the trees is thick and long, certainly tall enough to conceal a fugitive if he is lying prone, but again the troopers end up empty-handed. They even check the sparse canopies of the gnarled trees.

The search of the outbuildings is similarly unsuccessful. It turns up nothing more than some old bicycles leaning against one another in a corner of the barn. Flashlight beams play over the machines. Max's gaze follows the beams of light as he examines the scene with the Germans.

And sees what was never there before.

He glances around cautiously. The Feldkommandant and his men are registering nothing.

"Who owns these bicycles?" asks Wolff.

Max goes over to them.

"This one is mine. That one belonged to my wife. The others have been here for years. No one really owns them. I don't even know if all of them are still in working order. Do you want me to find out?"

Without waiting for a reply, he separates one of the machines and begins to wheel it towards Wolff. But the German has lost interest.

"You should lock them away, Monsieur. Bicycles are valuable. They will be stolen."

"I doubt that. The people of Dinon aren't thieves. They're not killers and they're not thieves."

He returns the bicycle to the corner with the others. The troopers show no more interest in it than Wolff did. They are bored and tired now, stifling their yawns. Their time and energy have been wasted. Their enthusiasm has waned. All they want is their beds. They are already turning away. Wolff orders them back to the trucks.

*   *   *

Max watches from the barn as the German vehicles depart, including Wolff's. The air remains pungent and oily with exhaust fumes.

The bicycle he offered to Wolff is as ancient and rusty as the others, but its saddle and handlebars, unlike theirs, are clean of grime, as clean as his own bicycle—evidence of recent use. Shreds of greenery are caught in its drive chain. The sort of thing that might happen if the rider had dumped it in undergrowth, carelessly or in great haste. A rider, say, who had then been obliged to retrieve it some while later. A rider, perhaps, very like the one Max saw scrambling down the railway embankment a few hours ago. And who then cycled past the Picardie only to be forced to return moments later, entering the grounds just seconds ahead of Egon Wolff and his men.

CHAPTER 7

ON THAT MIDSUMMER day when Wolff took possession of Dinon he was driven around his new fiefdom, dragging Max along with him in the rear of the armored car. The people of Dinon watched in stunned silence as German troops and their trucks and motorcycles and armed vehicles progressed through every street and square. If some point of interest caught Wolff's eye, he ordered a stop and leapt down from the vehicle for a closer look, to the consternation of citizens who found themselves suddenly confronted at close quarters by the German Reich in the flesh, complete with that disquieting facial disfigurement.

Wolff did everything at speed. He marched through the empty halls of the former college and decreed it suitable for conversion to barracks for his men. He supervised the handover—meaning seizure—of the town's firearms, a loss bitterly resented by Dinon's hunters and farmers.

"How are we to keep vermin down?" they protested. "The rats will devour everything. And we must be allowed to hunt. The right of every Frenchman to hunt dates back to the Revolution."

Wolff looked bored.

"Use traps," he told them. "Trapping was good enough for your forefathers before your Revolution. Traps and ferrets. You have another revolution now. Adapt."

*　　*　　*

He needed premises for his Kommandantur, his regional headquarters and administrative office. As soon as he saw the mairie in its commanding position overlooking Dinon's largest square, his decision was made.

"Perfect," he said. "There are empty rooms—no need for you to move out, Monsieur Duval. We will share the building. We will be neighbors. My Wehrmacht engineers will install our own radio and telegraph equipment alongside additional telephone lines. These will provide dedicated connections with Military High Command in Paris without interfering with civilian lines or requiring intervention by local switchboard operators. So you see, we will not be a burden to Dinon. You will hardly even know we are here."

"Tough on Laure Rioche," whispered Hortense. "No eavesdropping. Well, only on the rest of us, not on the Germans."

*　　*　　*

That left the matter of Wolff's personal accommodation.

He demanded to see the Hôtel Picardie, intrigued to learn of Max's ownership of the place. He fell silent as his vehicle left rue de la République and passed through the gateway, over the ramp and into the walled grounds, and the Picardie rose before him, its windows golden in the early evening light. In that silence Max sensed his interest.

The German paused to examine the heavy oak doors with their massive hinges and locks, he raised a bemused eyebrow at the portraits of Duc Henri and his ancestors; but he grunted in what Max took for approval of the comfortable lobby and dining room and library with their fine oak paneling.

In the best guest suite, he pulled coverlets aside without asking permission, removed a glove and ran his hand over the crisp bed linen.

He inspected Bruno's kitchen with its gleaming pots and pans and shining steel counters and ovens and hobs. Bruno watched him calmly, his arms folded over his massive chest, his white jacket crisp and spotless.

"Your name?" demanded Wolff.

Bruno gazed coolly down at him.

"Le Brun," he growled. "People call me Bruno."

"You will prepare dinner for me this evening," the German informed him. "I enjoy steak. I do not think you will try to poison me, Monsieur Bruno le Brun."

The gardens and grounds seemed to fascinate him. He stood before the maze, almost as if he was thinking about entering it.

"What's he up to?" muttered Bruno.

Max remembered the German's silence and stillness on his first glimpse of the Picardie. He remembered his amusement at the account of Duc Henri's fate—a carefully abbreviated version with no mention of ghosts.

"I think he wants to play seigneur, Bruno. He wants to be lord of the manor. I think he's planning to stay here."

"Out of the question!" The chef's moustache quivered with each expletive that followed. "We can't have the bastard living here."

"Take it easy, Bruno. Having him here could be exactly what we need."

"Or it could be the death of us."

"Make sure his steak's a good one. We'll play the hand we're dealt. We'll tug our forelocks and swear fealty like loyal serfs if that's what it takes."

"Do we have a choice?"

* * *

"I like this hotel of yours," Wolff told Max that evening. "It has everything I need and you run it to a high standard. My dinner was excellent. You have a good chef. I think your Hôtel Picardie will suit me perfectly. I think you will look after me. You will want to do that. It will be in your interests to do so. Yes?"

"Yes," agreed Max.

"Very good. It is settled. I will take the suite you showed me. A simple bedroom will suffice for my aide. You will be permitted to invoice my Kommandantur at half your usual tariff. You accept these terms, yes?"

"Yes," agreed Max again. In his mind's eye he touched an imaginary forelock.

CHAPTER 8

SHE DID NOT cut across the meadow. Doing so would have meant traveling blind into its darkness and unknown depths, since the map did not deal with the open countryside, only the streets and lanes and alleys of Dinon and the roads running into and from the town. There was no knowing what she might have found in the meadow or on its far side—or what might have found her. She could have blundered into another motorized patrol on some unexpected track or into troopers scouring the area on foot, moving invisibly through the darkness.

So she decided to stay here, in this wide grassy ditch—an old moat, she thinks—on the other side of the high wall enclosing the orchard; safer to lie here, she advised herself, silent and still, and wait for the Germans to pass by on the road.

But they did not pass by. They did not keep to the road. She heard their vehicles enter the grounds of this place after her and rattle into the same courtyard through which she had fled, she heard orders being shouted while to her horror what sounded like a whole squad of troopers leapt to the ground and began to spread out, their racket echoing in all directions. She could hear them tramping back and forth, probably into and out of the château. They had dogs; the animals barked excitedly as their handlers tried to calm them.

A full search was being conducted. She was trapped.

Above the wall, stray flashlight beams flicked skyward. Then suddenly the whole sky above the wall blossomed into light, as if every light bulb in every room of the mysterious château had been switched on, as if there was no such thing as a blackout. The Germans were leaving nothing to chance.

Her worst fear was the dogs. Repeatedly they came within a few meters of her as they rampaged through the orchard, whining and yelping, with only the wall separating them from her. That was when she was tempted to break cover and make a run for it through the meadow. But the animals failed to detect her—either they were badly trained or they needed something to go on, something they did not have, such as a piece of clothing. Her lost skirt, for example. That was a frightening realization.

So she did not break cover. Trembling like a cornered animal, she stayed where she was. It was all she could do.

And now it is Gérard who comes to her thoughts. Gérard, Maman, Papa—all of them, but her brother Gérard most of all, who was always there in every moment of her life that she can remember.

If only he had failed to obtain a gun. If only she had known of his plan and dissuaded him.

If only their little family, all four of them, had joined the exodus from Paris before the Germans arrived on that terrible day. How dearly she wishes that above all.

If only this, if only that. But there is no point wishing. What happened, happened. It will happen forever; she will see that morning repeated forever.

Her beautiful brother is dead. Maman and Papa are gone, almost certainly dead. The dead stay dead. No amount of wishing can change that.

CHAPTER 9

THE PICARDIE HAS returned to darkness, all the lights extinguished. Now it is the first pale glimmer of morning that the blackout blinds are blocking.

All around Max there is disarray, the chaos caused by the search. But clearing up can wait. He goes to the bar, to his usual place behind the counter. It is a proper zinc counter hammered out, shaped and polished in the old way, a silvery masterpiece. It always pleases him, somehow it never fails to have a calming effect on him. He places his hands on the cool surface and allows himself a moment in which to draw strength from the reassuring feel of its pattern beneath his palms.

The clock above the mirror ticks quietly.

Such peace in this moment.

The situation is bad; but he knows how much worse it could be. At least the events in Dinon did not involve the three men he has been told to expect. That was his greatest fear. But the figure he saw on the railway embankment, the person who entered the grounds of the Picardie, was not one of them. That figure had quite another mission.

It remains to be seen whether the men can still get through, with Dinon locked down, cordoned and crawling with Wolff's men—but

better that than for them to have been captured. Even their death—
which God forbid—would have been better than capture.

He bends down to the drawer concealed beneath the lowest shelf
under the counter, unlocks it and extracts the bundle of oiled cloth
within. Its weight in his hand is heavy and solid.

The night is over. And such a night. Hopefully the three men are
safe somewhere. But the fact is that there are consequences of the
night's events that have yet to play out. Egon Wolff will not rest
until the missing assassin is dead or captured. Repercussions, he
said; there will be repercussions for the killing of his men.

What repercussions?

And on whom will they fall?

Max unfolds the oiled cloth and removes the Browning
semi-automatic.

There will always be guns in Dinon.

He draws back the slide and loads a bullet into the chamber. The
metallic sound rings out loudly in the stillness of the empty
building.

So who is this killer bringing disaster and suffering upon Dinon?
It is time to find out.

*   *   *

Outside, the noise from the town has diminished. Max can still
hear vehicle engines in the distance, German voices are still shouting commands, but the clank of heavy machinery has ceased and
the vehicles are no longer revving at speed. It does not mean the
search is over; it only means that Wolff's roadblocks are now in
place, the cordon complete, and his armored vehicles and trucks
with armed troopers have taken up the positions they will hold for
the duration of his security operation.

According to what little information Max was able to extract from the Feldkommandant, house-to-house searches continued in the town throughout the night while Wolff was investigating the Picardie, and will be the business of this new day.

A hard night it has been for the people of Dinon, then. And with hard days to come. Possibly harder than any they have known.

Max goes to the orchard. It is not difficult to plot the assassin's probable route on entering the Picardie's grounds and the courtyard. He would have gone straight to the barn, an open structure with no doors to slow him down or keep him out. A few paces inside, to dump the bicycle.

From the barn, a few more paces would have brought him into the orchard and down here to its far end. Then over the wall to safety.

But wherever he is now, wherever he has spent the hours of darkness while the search was progressing, he will be back. He needs the bicycle.

And the chances are he will return the same way he left, and in the same place.

Max moves carefully through the nettles and tough grass, placing his feet carefully and stepping slowly so that the thick stems part silently.

The sky continues to brighten. A blackbird begins to sing, indifferent to Max's and Dinon's concerns, indifferent to assassins and occupiers and all of man's business of war. The song ascends like a prayer through the morning air. The trilling pauses, starts again. And again. Pure notes, rich melodies that soar and fall, little rivers of music, no phrase ever repeated exactly.

Max wonders what song it is. A song of territory? Or of innocent joy for being alive?

He wonders if his intruder is listening with him.

When scuffling noises sound on the other side of the wall, he is ready. He flattens himself against the rough stonework.

Two hands appear at the top of the wall, grasping it so that their owner can haul himself across its width. The hands become a pair of dark-sleeved forearms. They remain stationary for a time. Max guesses that the man is looking around to check he is safe.

Then, as agile as a cat, he lands on all fours directly in front of Max, his back to him. Before the intruder can rise to his feet, Max has closed on him from behind and is pressing the snout of the Browning to the back of his head, immediately below the black beret he is wearing.

The man freezes. He expels a sigh—a sound of frustration or irritation, it seems to Max, or possibly anger; certainly not fear.

"Hands on your head. Don't stand up."

The man obeys. The hands rise, the upper half of his body straightens but his knees remain on the ground. Still behind him, Max passes his hands quickly over the man's clothing, searching for weapons. He finds a jackknife, a small Beretta pistol, a spare magazine, some cash and an identity card. The pistol is old and looks badly maintained. It is not a weapon he would trust or want to stake his life on, but the acrid smell of spent powder tells him it has been fired recently.

He pockets the Beretta and the other items. He will examine the identity card later.

He turns his attention back to his captive. Something is not right; something about this figure kneeling before him is not right.

That narrow back. The jacket that hangs so loosely on the shoulders. The trousers with their waistband turned on itself, where he found the Beretta. Badly fitting clothing is nothing unusual these days but this man seems to be an extreme case.

There is something else—those hands, so slim and fine-boned.

The man's head is bowed, as if he is studying the ground. All that Max can see of him is the black beret. And the back of his neck. That slim neck.

And when he ran his hands over the man's clothing . . .

Suddenly he understands. He snatches the beret away. A cascade of dark hair tumbles free. The head lifts, turns towards him, and a pair of gray eyes gaze up at him. Eyes burning with defiance.

Eyes that, in another time and place, could steal a man's soul.

CHAPTER 10

He takes her at gunpoint out of the orchard, past the barn and the garage block and into the Picardie. She remains silent and he speaks only to direct her steps. He steers her to the lobby and through its confusion—chairs and tables toppled, floor rugs kicked into heaps. In the half-light it is an obstacle course that she might try to use to her advantage, so he never takes his eyes off her. He has seen her physical capability in the ease with which she scaled the orchard wall; here among the shadows and disorder is where she might be foolhardy enough to attempt an escape—because for all she knows, he could be about to hand her over to the Germans.

Under his instructions she raises the blinds, going from window to window. Daylight pours in. She looks around, taking in Max and her surroundings. She shows no sign of being cowed or intimidated; indeed, he could be the intruder rather than she. When she sees the array of portraits along the oak- paneled walls of the lobby, especially Duc Henri's, her lips compress with scorn.

Max nods towards an upended chair.

"Pick it up."

But she has had enough of following his orders. She shoves her hands into her pockets.

"Pick it up yourself. I'm not your servant and you're no aristocrat. I'm not here to do your bidding."

Her words are disdainful but she is softly spoken and the pitch of her voice is low. An educated voice.

He raises the Browning in response to her refusal. She utters a derisive snort but picks up the chair all the same and places it where he indicates, near the tall windows.

He glances out at the familiar view: the untidy grounds, the empty road. From here he can watch for anyone approaching, although Wolff is unlikely to return to the Picardie until tonight; he will be busy supervising the search operation in Dinon.

Max assesses his captive. She is not from Dinon; he has never seen her before. She is young, perhaps twenty or so, and she has all the boldness of youth, for as he studies her he is conscious that she is examining him just as candidly. Something in her gaze makes him uneasy; he has seen its like before somewhere.

She is tall and lightly built. The gray eyes might be flecked with other colors, but it is hard to be sure because he is unwilling to engage with them for any length of time. Too dangerous.

She would stand out in any civilized company. But civilized company is not available today. And today she is a sorry sight. There are dark rings of exhaustion under those eyes, streaks of dirt and sweat on her face. Her hands are bloodied and criss-crossed with cuts. Her clothing is torn and littered with leaves and debris.

This is no seasoned fighter, no skilled assassin. And now she has become his problem. He cannot let her fall into Wolff's hands. Her way of resistance is not his but the two of them are on the same side and share the same foe.

But neither can he guard her through every hour she will have to spend here. The Picardie is not a jail and he cannot be her jailer; he must be able to leave her and know she will not do anything that could attract Wolff's attention. She has done enough damage already with her stupid escapade.

He nudges the chair with his foot, angling it away from the windows.

"Sit there."

She makes a performance of settling herself comfortably, unhurriedly, arranging the oversized jacket and stretching her legs as if taking her place at an elegant soirée. But at least she has obeyed. He keeps his distance from her and remains standing.

"So you're responsible for what happened last night. You and your comrade."

No answer other than a nonchalant shrug. She uses the beret, as battered as the rest of her clothing, to brush leaves from her trousers.

"Let's be clear," he continues. "I don't approve of what you've done, but I'm not your enemy and I have no intention of turning you over to the Germans. I don't want you here but if you try to leave now, you'll never make it to safety. Do you understand?"

She is watching him from behind the curtain of hair. She still offers no response.

He continues. "You give me a problem by dumping yourself on my doorstep—"

She raises her head abruptly, pushes her hair out of the way.

"If you're not going to turn me in, if you're not my enemy, you don't need that gun."

"I need it until I'm sure you won't do anything stupid."

"Really? What do you think I might do? What *can* I do? You've disarmed me. In fact, nothing you say makes any sense—you won't turn me in but apparently you might shoot me. What kind of logic is that? You don't want me here but you're the one who's stopping me leaving. Seems to me you need to make your mind up."

She places her hands on her knees and sits forward as though to rise from the chair. He raises the Browning. She ignores it.

"Just let me go on my way," she tells him. "It's as easy as that. That solves everything."

"I'm keeping you here for your own safety."

"Are you? How do I know what to believe? And by the way, I didn't dump myself on you—it's your own fault I'm here. You could have stayed out of this, you and your hotel or whatever this place is. If it wasn't for you, I'd be gone by now."

"And blundering straight into the hands of the Germans."

She sits back in the chair. "So what? Why should you care? Why are you interfering?"

"I'm helping you."

"Why?"

"I have my reasons."

"And they are?"

He disregards the question and takes her identity card from his pocket.

"Let's see who you are. Or at any rate who you're pretending to be."

He examines the card. The photograph is certainly of her—the face a little younger but the same bold gaze. There is a genuine-looking police stamp, Seine département, and the address details and other sections are properly filled in.

And here is her date of birth. Apparently she turned twenty just a few months ago. That much at least is probably true.

"So you're calling yourself Sophie Carrière. Paris address. I assume the card's a forgery. It's good work."

"Assume what you like." She has slipped into the familiar form of speech. "Now that we've been introduced, may I call you Max?"

For a moment he is thrown, then he sees that she is gazing at the reception desk, where his name is displayed. When he looks back at her, there is amusement in the gray eyes. She has enjoyed her little game.

So she has his name. No matter. If she is captured, she will lead the Germans here whether or not she knows his name. He took that risk the moment he apprehended her.

"Your accomplice is dead," he says. "Did you know?"

She is serious now. "Jean-Luc was a brave man. He died for France. And now it's time for you to give me back that identity card and my other belongings. You have no right to keep them."

But he puts the card back in his pocket. She sighs, shakes her head wearily.

"Do you have any idea how much trouble you're causing, Sophie Carrière from Paris?"

Wide-eyed irony now. "That was the general idea, Max Duval from Dinon."

"Trouble for the Germans, yes. But I'm talking about the danger you're putting others in."

She tilts her head in mock sympathy. "So you're annoyed because you're in danger."

"This isn't about me. It's about the many others you've endangered. You've taken no account of them. You're too busy being heroic—or what you think is heroic—too busy playing the hero to think of that."

"I'm fighting for France, Max, that's what I'm doing. You should try it sometime."

"Your motives may be noble, but the same can't be said of those who sent you."

"How would you know?"

"Because they've been here. I've met them. Communists and killers. They were here and talked the night away. They're good at talking. A recruitment drive, you might call it—but an unsuccessful one, I sent them packing. They'd like Dinon to take up arms with them. It's time for us all to become killers like them, that's what they say. They'd like us to provide them with more Sophies and Jean-Lucs."

"And if you haven't, why is that?"

"Why should we send more like you to their deaths? Why should we waste more lives? There are other ways."

"Other ways to resist? Tell me what they are, I'd dearly like to know. No? You have nothing to say? That's because you're just making excuses for doing nothing, for not fighting back against the Germans. I call that collaboration."

The accusation does not surprise him. He knew it would come, sooner or later. The privilege of youth, to distill the complex to simplicity, as though simplicity is clarity.

"I call it living peaceably with them, Sophie—and it's why none of our citizens has died at their hands. We don't provoke them and it works. We intend to keep it that way."

She is giving him the same look she bestowed on Duc Henri. "Then it's true what we hear in Paris—Dinon is full of collaborators."

He shakes his head. "Not collaborators, just ordinary people trying to survive. Trying to be safe, trying to feed their children. They make the best decisions they can, day by day, one small decision at a time."

"Instead of behaving like sheep, they should look for ways to undermine the Germans."

"And some do, in whatever ways they can. Small ways only, undramatic and not very heroic by your standards. Small acts that inconvenience the Germans. In fact, you couldn't have come here without the help of at least one of those people. Think about that bicycle you used, the one you hid in my barn." He sees her surprise at his knowledge. "I'd say you came by train to Rue and then cycled the rest of the way here. But you didn't bring the bicycle with you from Paris—that could have drawn attention to you on the train. Someone from Dinon left it in a prearranged place for you to collect. And another one for your friend Jean-Luc."

She neither confirms nor denies his reasoning, but she is watching and listening attentively.

"That person risked their life in doing that," he continues. "Bear that example in mind when you call us collaborators. As for the men who sent you here, on the other hand—their motives aren't as pure as you believe."

She pushes her hair out of the way again; doing so seems to be a habit. She frowns.

"What are you saying?"

"You need to understand what will happen because of last night. Resistance actions like yours have consequences. The Germans will exact vengeance. Dinon will be punished for what you did. The local Feldkommandant has said as much. There'll be reprisals— arrests, maybe interrogations in an attempt to find out who helped you and who might know your identity or where you're hiding. That's how the Germans start. There could be worse to come."

"Such as?"

But she already knows. It is in those gray eyes from which all amusement has now vanished. She folds the beret and rests it in her lap, studies her hands with their scratches and cuts. She is not so sure of herself now.

"Innocent people will pay for what you've done, people who have nothing to do with you or your leaders and who had no say in what you did last night. The Germans aren't fussy—they don't care who suffers provided it makes their point and gets them what they want."

She is very still.

"Here's the worst of it. You and your comrade were sent here precisely to trigger those reprisals—because your leaders think that will finally make Dinon join them. You've been manipulated. That's why you're here. Not to strike a blow for freedom but to push Dinon into doing what it doesn't want to do."

"No—"

"Puppets, you and Jean-Luc, that's what you are. Your leaders in Paris are the ones pulling your strings. You danced at the end of those strings all the way from Paris to Dinon."

Her face is flushed with anger. Perhaps there is also the pain of hearing the truth.

"You're wrong."

"Look at the facts. Two dead Germans—"

Her head snaps up. "Not two. I only wounded the one I shot. My gun jammed."

"Well, he died. Those men were just ordinary soldiers. Not even senior officers. Just ordinary men with families."

"Our fighters have families. So do all French citizens. Do you think I didn't have a family once?"

So she has known loss. He notes the point.

"But why send you and Jean-Luc all the way here to kill two unimportant soldiers? You could have killed men like them in Paris—and more easily and more safely. So why bother coming to Dinon? Your leaders didn't even make sure you had a proper escape plan. You were supposed to be on that freight train from here last night, weren't you? Yes—I know about it as well."

"I was late. My own fault."

"Or was it a useless plan from the start? Evidently it was a plan with no fallback. That makes it your leaders' fault—every bit as much as the useless gun they gave you is their fault. Listen to me, Sophie Carrière. In the same way as innocent people in Dinon will suffer in the Germans' reprisals, you and your comrade were set up as sacrifices. Jean-Luc is already dead and it doesn't matter if you die as well—your leaders won't care. All that matters to them is Dinon taking up arms. They don't need either of you to return alive, and in some ways it's all the better if you don't—they can sing your praises as martyrs for the cause."

"Martyrs?"

"Like Jean-Luc. You said it yourself—a brave man who gave his life for France. Martyrs are always useful. Now tell me this— did either of you already know Dinon? Had you been here previously?"

"No, but our briefing was good—we had a good map and exact directions."

Another point for him to note. Where did the map and directions come from?

"How many assassination missions have you been on before last night?"

She looks away, embarrassed. "Last night was my first."

"And Jean-Luc?"

"They told me he was experienced."

"They *told* you? So you only had their word for that, and neither of you was familiar with this area. You hadn't worked together before and neither of you knew Dinon."

"Nothing's perfect. We all have to start somewhere."

"Yes—but start on your own home ground, on familiar territory. Start in Paris."

"It's vital to take the fight beyond Paris, it has to be all of France."

He hears the hard men, the communists and killers, in the ready-made line. She is parroting them. Egon Wolff has no monopoly on propaganda.

"We learn as we go along," she adds.

"This isn't a parlor game. Do you think the Germans settle for learning as they go along?"

She seems not to have heard. Or to have heard only too well. Her gaze is fixed on the floor.

"Sophie?"

She gives a start and looks up at him.

"You'll do nothing stupid?" he asks. "Do I still need this gun?"

Another of her shrugs, a minimal motion as if the matter is hardly worth her attention.

"That's up to you, Max. You're the one with all the answers."

He uncocks the Browning and puts it away.

She is tough. Behind the exhaustion and dirt he sees the determination that made her a perfect candidate for last night's operation.

But perhaps he has drummed some sense into her. Perhaps he has brought her under control for as long as she must remain here.

Under control and out of his way.

He reflects on what he has told her and what he has learnt from her. He was right about the bicycle: someone in Dinon supplied it. Two bicycles, in fact. He has not misled her or exaggerated: serious risks were taken in getting both machines to a hiding place and concealing them there. Two machines may have meant two journeys. Double the risk.

That same someone or another willing helper supplied the map and directions with which she and Jean-Luc navigated Dinon's streets and lanes. Evening curfew with no passenger trains running would have meant that the pair had to hide themselves somewhere between their arrival at Rue and the attack in Dinon several hours later. Someone provided them with that hiding place, or at the very least told them where to find a safe spot.

All of which points to local support throughout their ill-conceived enterprise—support that provided both logistical help and detailed local knowledge that the hard men in Paris would not have possessed.

So someone in Dinon is in very close communication with those men. Who is that someone? And what else might follow from their alliance with the hard men?

He has no intention of waiting to find out. It is time for that someone to stop. Or be stopped.

The landscape outside the lobby windows has remained deserted. But now a lone cyclist is laboring up the incline of rue de la République towards the Picardie.

No mistaking that great brawny figure. Bruno is on his way.

"You'll come with me now, Sophie Carrière or whoever you really are."

"Come with you where?"

"Where you'll be safe."

"Why should I trust you?"

"You won't, no matter what I say. But you'll come anyway."

She sighs. "So it's you or the Germans. Occupiers or collaborators—not much of a choice."

She shoves the beret into a pocket. As she rises from the chair, the gray eyes light on him.

There it is, that defiant gaze of hers, unclouded by doubt. And suddenly he knows where he has met its like before.

It is how Geneviève faced the world.

CHAPTER 11

TEN MINUTES LATER he crosses the courtyard again, his destination the barn. Bruno has put his bicycle with the others, in the same corner that was almost the scene of Max's—and therefore Sophie's—undoing. As Max approaches, he stands gazing at the machines while he begins to roll a cigarette.

He looks unhappily at Max, a dark look that contains both regret and anger. "I guess you heard the gunfire last night. Wolff certainly did—it brought him into Dinon on the rampage."

"I understand there were two gunmen but one was killed."

"The other one's on the loose. Wolff's out to get him."

"Well, he didn't confine his attentions to the town. He came back here to search."

Now there is alarm in the chef's face. "He searched the Picardie?"

"Don't worry—he found nothing. I wouldn't be here if he'd found anything. There was nothing to find—nothing and no one. They didn't show up."

Bruno exhales a long breath. "Under the circumstances, thanks be to God for small mercies."

"I'm not surprised they didn't make it—it would have been impossible for them to get through."

"Where do you suppose they are now?"

'Still safe with their guides, I hope.'

'So—what do we do?'

"We wait. The guides will try again when it's safe. Does anyone in Dinon know anything about the gunmen?"

"Only that they don't seem to be from Dinon—there are no reports of anyone missing or unaccounted for. Several people claim to have seen the surviving gunman escaping, but I've heard nothing to suggest anyone recognized him. He could be halfway across France by now, but Wolff is continuing to search in Dinon. Basically, we have a full-scale manhunt on our hands."

"The last thing we need."

Bruno scratches unhappily at his moustache. "It's bad, Max. Dinon's a disaster. Wolff is ripping it to pieces. Also outlying areas. People can't get to work or aren't showing up because their homes have been wrecked. Wolff calls it a search but it's being done with malice."

"He has to answer to avenue Kléber, Military High Command in Paris, for last night. It's a stain on his record, a personal affront to him."

"Well, he's taking it out on Dinon. Businesses are at a standstill. There isn't even bread—the boulangerie hasn't been able to open. All the roads have barriers manned by armed troopers. I had to pass through three roadblocks to get here. You can't move for Boche, they're everywhere—there are so many of the bastards when they're all out of barracks at the same time. They ransacked my house. People are frightened and there's anger, real anger, because of how our Feldkommandant is handling the situation. I tell you, Max— you'll have your work cut out to calm people down and reassure them."

"I'll go into town this morning. You won't like it when you see what's been done to your kitchen."

"It's only a kitchen."

After many pauses along the way, Bruno has finished assembling his cigarette. As he puts it between his lips and digs out a match he turns back to the cluster of bicycles. He prods one of them with his toe. Max watches. The machine is Sophie's.

"Whose bicycle is this, Max? I don't recognize it. It can't be one of ours."

Max's silence makes Bruno turn to look at him.

"Max?"

"We have company."

Bruno's hand holding the match stops in mid-air. He frowns. "But you said no one—"

"I know what I said."

Bruno strikes the match, lights the cigarette, and takes a deep first drag as he weighs Max's words. Max gives him time to absorb the situation, or as much of it as he can work out for himself.

"Damnation!"

The chef whispers the word through a cloud of smoke. He scans the courtyard as though Wolff and a phalanx of troopers might be lying in wait.

"The gunman escaped by bicycle. Are you telling me he's here, Max? Here, in the Picardie? Have you allowed him to hide here? What have you done? What are you getting us involved in? We always said—*you* said—we wouldn't have anything to do with these people. They're killers. They proved that last night. It's crazy—this man is one of theirs."

Max produces the identity card.

"Not a man, Bruno."

* * *

Max's private quarters, at the end of that winding corridor along which Wolff's clumsy farm boys tramped some hours earlier, are safely distant from the guest and public areas of the hotel. When Max brought Sophie here, he quickly cleared the photographs away from the bedside table, wanting no repeat of his experience with Egon Wolff. He provided her with fresh bed linen and towels, but the only clothes available were his own: he gave Geneviève's away long ago, when he could no longer bear their presence. He could never have allowed Sophie to have them anyway; it is difficult enough to think of her in the bed where he and Geneviève slept.

He knocks on the door, waits until he hears her respond, then unlocks the door and enters. She is standing by the bedroom's one small window. Its view is limited to a corner of the courtyard and a section of what was in Duc Henri's day a row of stables and is now the garage block. It is hardly a picturesque view, but he sees that this is of no concern to her; it is the sliver of daylight she wants, even though the room's single electric light is on. His shaving mirror is propped on the windowsill. She has bathed and dressed, and is using her fingers to comb through her hair, her head tipped forward.

As he enters, she stops, tosses her hair back, straightens up and turns to face him. She is wearing a pair of his rough corduroy trousers and a collarless shirt, still damp here and there from her body. Like her previous attire, the garments are too large. Even so, the shirt clings to her form, hinting at the rise of her breasts. She is barefoot, her boots now scraped clean and placed neatly by the bed. For all her bluster and bravado there is something vulnerable in those bare feet. Her beret, washed now even if still stained, is hanging on the back of the door to dry.

The room is fragrant with the smell of soap—his soap but he has never been aware of its fragrance before.

"How long are you going to keep me here?" she demands.

"Until it's safe. Not just safe for you—you'll stay until it's safe for everyone affected by what you've done."

"When will that be?"

"I'll let you know."

His answer does not please her but it shuts her up.

He has brought a tray with coffee and some croissants—yesterday's croissants but there was nothing else, and he has warmed them. As he sets the tray down on the small table, he notes that she has bundled up her clothing as he instructed, so that it can be incinerated—a precaution in case she is described by any witnesses in Dinon. It is a possibility now made more tangible by Bruno's report that her escape was seen. The bundle is waiting on the bed.

The aroma of the coffee reaches her.

"Is that coffee? You have proper coffee?"

"There's a reason. And it's important that you understand what it is."

Her gaze is still on the tray and its contents. He wonders when she last ate.

"What reason?" she asks.

"This hotel receives special classification by the Ministry of Provisions. Hence the coffee and some other benefits in terms of food rations. Our status means you're safer here than anywhere else in Dinon. We're not subject to random raids, and the local police leave us alone. Naturally there are limits—we were searched last night, like everywhere else. But that was an exceptional circumstance—thanks to you. So unless you cause another such exception, I don't expect that to happen again. And I hope you'll see to it that there is no further exception."

Her gaze has moved from the tray. She has been watching him with growing suspicion.

"So why this special status?"

"It's because of certain guests who are resident here. They're also why you must stay out of sight. They're the Feldkommandant of this region and—"

She steps back as if physically assaulted. Her eyes blaze. "No!"

"Yes, whether you like it or not—the same man who's hunting for you. Other Reich personnel and French civilians on Reich business also take rooms here from time to time."

"You're telling me you have Germans living here? Under your own roof? And collaborators! Do you accommodate these scum for free or do you take their blood money? All your talk about survival—this is out-and-out collaboration, and far worse than I thought. You tried to set me against my leaders—I was even starting to believe you—but all the while you're in the Germans' pockets!"

"This is the real world, Sophie, where people don't go storming about the countryside killing Germans. You're the one who chose to hide yourself in the Picardie."

She has been padding back and forth in the restricted space of the bedroom as her anger grows. Now she pushes the tray aside, almost sliding it off the table.

"Take this away. I don't want your filthy coffee. It would choke me. It's as disgusting as you are. It would choke any decent French citizen. Save it for your German masters."

He picks up the bundle of clothing but leaves the tray. He stops at the door and looks back at her.

"That window, Sophie—however you feel about being here, remember what I said about staying out of sight. My German masters, as you call them, they keep their vehicle over there in the old stable block. Don't let yourself be seen. Be as angry as you like but don't get careless."

She is staring at her reflection in the mirror as if trying to understand how she has ended up in this situation. But as he opens the door she finds her voice.

"My name really is Sophie Carrière. It's not a false name. The identity card is genuine, not a forgery."

He shakes his head in puzzlement at this information. "If that's true, I can't think of anything more foolish. But why are you telling me this now? Why tell me at all?"

"It's for when you betray me and hand me over to your Feldkommandant. I know you'll do that in the end. When they execute me, I want my name to be on your conscience. I'll be what you said—a martyr for France. And when France is free again, I want you to remember my name then as well, when it's your turn to face the firing squad—as the collaborator that you are."

* * *

He goes to the kitchen.

"Keep an eye on her for me today, Bruno. See if you can persuade her to eat something. She should eat."

He receives an unenthusiastic grunt by way of reply. It might mean yes; it might mean no. But he is familiar with Bruno's moods; no use arguing with him.

He takes the clothing to the basement, opens the door of the stove and thrusts the bundle inside.

He thought he had drummed some sense into her, but now he is not so sure. He seems to have undone his own efforts. But she has to understand the Picardie's unique position—or at least as much of that as he can allow.

He may be making a very big mistake. Those who sent her here, the hard men, are reckless; it is clear that they have no real understanding of security. What kind of leaders send their people—to all intents and purposes untrained—on a mission without fake identities, without a good escape plan, and with a gun that jams?

"We learn as we go along."

Why is he taking it upon himself to protect her when her own leaders have failed to do so? And with such leadership as her example, can she be trusted in any way at all?

Perhaps Bruno is right; perhaps he should never have intervened. She is tough, but she may also turn out to be more dangerous than he could have imagined. Difficult and dangerous.

He watches as the clothing burns.

CHAPTER 12

HE DOES WHAT he can to set the lobby, dining room, library and bar to rights.

Young Paul the kitchen lad arrives, close to tears as he describes how his mother's apartment, their shared home, was raided during the night. Virginie the housekeeper, when she arrives, is spitting with fury, her cottage also having been searched. She swears with gusto when she sees what has been done to her polished floors and spotless rugs here in the Picardie, and, most inexcusable of all, her immaculate linen.

"Wolff isn't a normal human person, Monsieur Max. Something's wrong in him. Something's missing. God forgot something."

Paul joins Bruno in the kitchen. Virginie goes off to deal with the guest rooms. Provided Sophie does nothing to draw attention to her presence, neither of them will happen upon her—they never venture to Max's quarters, which are well away from anywhere their day's work will take them.

It is time for him to go into Dinon. Time to see what Wolff and his men have done to his town.

Time also to deal with another matter that has been on his mind. Which is why he does not take his own bicycle. He leaves it in the barn and takes Sophie's instead.

* * *

Exactly as Bruno said, Wolff's troopers are everywhere, even on the outskirts of town, where Max sees them fanning across fields with their dogs, searching farmhouses, barns, sheds, outhouses.

He has not gone far on rue de la République when he meets the first roadblock—a barrier with warning notices in German and French, and beside it a truck with five or six armed troopers already sweating in the sun. Their dogs rise up and growl at him, straining at their chains. It will be another hot day and the tempers of dogs and men will become shorter as the mercury rises.

The troopers demand his identity card and take their time examining it. Everything is done by the book; and today their book is a grindingly laborious one. Then come the questions, asked and answered in a mix of their garbled French and his inept German: where is he coming from, where was he last night, where is he going this morning, with what purpose?

The same performance is repeated on each of the two subsequent occasions he is stopped. The blank faces of the Germans and the slowness with which everything is done are the same, as if Wolff's troopers are all cast from the same mold, like toy soldiers. But exasperating and dangerous toy soldiers.

Despite Bruno's warning, Max is shocked when he sees what has been done to Dinon. And what is still being done.

He has always considered his town beautiful. And it *was* beautiful, until the Germans came. They have blighted that beauty, obliterated it. They suspended huge scarlet banners of the German Reich with their black swastikas from every public building, including the mairie, to Hortense's horror, and any structure able to accommodate them—the water tower, warehouses. They put new road and street signs in position, spelling out directions and names in their ugly Gothic lettering.

Soon Egon Wolff's propaganda was everywhere: posters featuring the face of his Führer, posters warning of the dangers posed by Jews, posters promoting the trusty German soldier as a friend to all, posters about the joys of working in Germany, posters condemning the Resistance, posters warning against communists and Bolsheviks. Posters for every imaginable and objectionable purpose. And always a steady spew of notices spelling out the latest new laws and ordinances.

The sheer physical presence of the Germans is unrelenting and inescapable. It is not only a matter of when they are carrying out their duties. Off duty, they are just as intrusive. On summer days they swim in the Authie and sunbathe and practice callisthenics on its banks, showing off their healthy, well-fed bodies. They are wherever the eye might glance, wherever the head turns. Their brash voices and laughter fill the air, too loud and too confident.

Just as Hortense says, there is no getting away from them. They are there every minute of every day, their vehicles belching smoke, their deafening motorcycles weaving everywhere, a feldgrau infestation that drains the color from every scene. It is as though Egon Wolff and his Reich have not only stolen France from the French; they have erased beauty itself from the world.

But today is worse than all of that. Today insult is being added to injury. Today every building Max passes, whether business premises or residential, has had its contents tipped into the street. Wolff's men are still busy adding to the chaos. Sometimes there is barely room for Max to weave through the confusion.

Furniture has been smashed. Mattresses have been ripped open. Household goods are strewn everywhere. Files of documents litter the street outside the notary's office. Retailers' stock, pathetically limited anyway, has been flung out and trampled.

There is a continuous backdrop of noise—the churning and roaring of vehicle engines, motorcycles revving, German voices always shouting as if normal speech volume is not possible, protests of the townspeople, children wailing. The Germans' dogs bark constantly. Local dogs challenge them, leading to more shouts and curses from the troopers and piercing yelps when a German boot sends a Dinon dog on its way.

Again, Bruno was right—there is deliberate heartlessness, a vindictiveness, in the way the search is being carried out. After a year of German occupation the people of Dinon have little enough left to them in the way of worldly goods and comforts; and now even that little is being ruined, consciously and methodically.

Nor did Bruno exaggerate the number of Germans engaged in the operation. Max has never seen so many in his town at one time. A gray plague, like rats. As well as the troopers engaged in the search, there are many more than normal on foot patrol, all of them in twos and threes rather than singly, and more armored vehicles crawling slowly along or squatting at corners and junctions, their occupants watching from slit observation windows or manning roof-mounted machine guns.

Max dismounts and walks through the streets and small squares, wheeling the bicycle by his side, always keeping it visible. People come to talk with him, sharing their tales of woe. Troopers glare at them, and for once the people glare back. On this, too, Bruno is right: there is an anger in the town that will be hard to assuage; it is as palpable as the rising heat of the morning.

Outside the pharmacy, a small, wiry woman is salvaging what she can from the confusion of items spread over the pavement. This is Juliette Labarthe, the pharmacist. As Max reaches her she straightens up, presses her hands to the small of her back and stretches.

"Not as young as I was, Max."

They embrace, cheek to cheek. Some troopers passing nearby pause to watch them.

"Pierre called on me yesterday," she tells Max quietly. The background noise keeps her words from the troopers.

"There's been no one yet, Juliette. They couldn't make it. We have to wait."

She sighs. "All because of some trigger-happy idiots."

She removes her spectacles and polishes them on her white coat. The troopers are moving on. They make no attempt to avoid stepping on the goods scattered all around.

"Wolff's doing more than looking for the wanted man," she says. "He's using the shooting as an excuse to search for anything illegal or incriminating—guns, wireless sets, anything that would justify punishing the town. God help us if he finds anything he thinks is connected with the Resistance." She gives Max a meaningful look. "A radio transmitter, for example. What he's doing now is nothing compared to how he'd respond to something like that."

Max nods slowly. He knows that Juliette's words are half warning and half question.

"Wolff won't find anything," he says. "No transmitter."

She accepts the reassurance. But there is more on her mind.

"We're not a Resistance town, Max—not that kind of Resistance, the armed kind." She replaces the spectacles and blinks up at him. "But if Wolff keeps on in this way, we both know what will happen."

"Don't say that, Juliette. You know where talk like that could lead."

"Of course I do, and I don't want it any more than you do. But look around you. You can see and hear how these people are feeling. They can't tolerate this. If Wolff carries on, the guns will come out—and there'll be fools ready and willing to use them. Then the Germans will hit back and the losers will be the innocent people of Dinon."

She clasps Max's hands briefly and goes back to rescuing what she can from the ground. He parks the bicycle against a telegraph pole and crouches down to the task with her, gathering together packets of tablets and dark bottles of mysterious liquids.

Over their efforts, over everyone and everything, Germans and Dinonnais alike, occupiers and occupied, flutter the scarlet banners and black swastikas of Wolff's glorious Reich.

Max ponders Juliette's warning. He thinks about Sophie Carrière, a far greater prize for Wolff than any radio transmitter. He thinks again about the risk he is taking in sheltering her—and putting others at risk in doing so.

It is the very crime of which he has accused her.

He continues on his way towards the mairie, a slow progress given the number of people who come to him or with whom he stops to talk or lend a helping hand. Always he is conscious of their anger, even if it remains unspoken.

He is in conversation with the foreman of the town's granary when he has the sensation of being watched. When he looks around he finds that a boy of nine or ten is standing nearby, staring hard at him; to be exact, staring at the bicycle.

"That's my uncle's bicycle," the boy says. "What are you doing with it?"

Max finishes with the foreman and goes over to the boy.

"I found it and didn't know whose it was," he explains. "But I know who you are—and I know who your uncle is. You're sure it's his?"

He fishes in his pocket, comes up with a few coins. The boy saunters off, whistling cheerfully, a little wealthier for the encounter.

To Max's chagrin, the ownership of the bicycle is as he suspected.

He comes to the surgery. Pierre's bicycle is there, so either he has not gone on his calls this morning or he has returned. The Chinese mannequin is in the window, its left arm and hand raised in its normal greeting, its coolie hat straight. So, no fresh developments overnight, no new information.

Today the little figure is watching the world with a frown, as if burdened with some weighty knowledge.

And perhaps it is, for the surgery has not escaped Wolff's ravages. Pierre's receptionist is patiently gathering folders and their contents from the road and pavement. Max stops to help.

"Pierre's gone to the mairie," she tells him.

"Looking for me?"

"No, he's gone there because—well, you'll see why. Don't ask me to describe it, Max. I've been trying to put it from my mind. You need to see for yourself."

CHAPTER 13

HE FINDS TWENTY or so people gathered outside the mairie. They are staring at something on the wall. As he comes closer he sees that a poster has been put up beside the noticeboard. Whatever it is, it could not have a more prominent position. But it is not something on which anyone wants to linger. They move off when they have seen enough, which does not take long, giving way to others who arrive to take their places. Heads shake, eyes are downcast. No one speaks above a whisper.

Pierre is standing off to one side, watching as the people come and go. He sees Max and comes across to him. His face is grim.

"Look what the German is doing now," he says. "Our Feldkommandant has excelled himself."

The poster features a grainy, life-sized photograph of a young man's head and shoulders. It is in full color. The face is pale, almost as white as the paper on which the image is printed. It is obvious that the man is dead, despite the open eyes.

The poster permits him no dignity in death. His jaw is slack, the lips are parted to reveal teeth set in a grimace. The hair is matted with a dark substance that is surely blood. Max realizes that this is Sophie's accomplice. He remembers the name: Jean-Luc.

The text in the poster describes Jean-Luc as one of the assassins of two brave soldiers of the Reich in Dinon. It commands that anyone recognizing him must report to the Kommandantur, to provide details of his identity.

The man had an accomplice, the poster says, and he is wanted for the same crime but has so far evaded capture. Anyone providing shelter or protection for this escaped killer will be deemed complicit in the assassins' crime and dealt with according to Reich law. The same will apply to anyone withholding information of any kind on either man. The penalty in all cases will be death.

"This won't achieve anything," says Pierre as he and Max move away to speak privately.

"You think not?"

"Of course not. I don't recognize this poor soul. Do you? So he's not from Dinon. The killings were the work of outsiders. We both know who. Even if someone in Dinon does know anything, which I doubt, who would dare inform on them? No, this won't get Wolff anywhere."

Max remembers Wolff's anger and his determination to hunt the assassin down—without mercy, without regrets—in the name of German honor. He will not give up easily.

"Then he'll try something else, Pierre. Military High Command will see that he does."

"Something else? What would that be?"

"I don't know. Nothing good."

At that moment the double doors shared by the Kommandantur and the mairie swing open and Egon Wolff appears. The little group of people quickly disperses. Pierre touches Max's arm by way of farewell and departs in the direction of his surgery.

Wolff greets Max with a nod. He remains on the top step, blocking the way to the mairie.

"Good morning, Monsieur le Maire. I am pleased to see you are catching up with my appeal for information. Do you recognize this murderer?"

"No, and I wouldn't expect to. He's not from Dinon—precisely as I told you."

"So you know the face of every citizen of Dinon? The poster will be widely displayed. Someone in your town knows who this enemy of the Reich is. They know his accomplice and where he can be found."

"What your men are doing to our homes and businesses is intolerable. You said nothing last night about the destruction this search of yours would cause. Either you deliberately misled me or you're failing to control your men. Neither is acceptable."

Wolff remains unconcerned. "Inconvenience is a fact of war. Dinon has brought this inconvenience upon itself."

"What you're doing is exactly what will drive Dinon into the arms of the enemy you want to eliminate. I don't want that—and you don't want it either."

Wolff is unimpressed. He descends the steps and walks past Max. His armored car is waiting for him by the curb. In the lane beside the mairie, his aide, smoking as usual in his favored spot, extinguishes his cigarette.

"Major, I intend to make a formal complaint against you. I'll be writing to avenue Kléber today. I'll also be seeking material restitution for the damage your actions have caused. I consider that a necessary first step if we're to stand any chance of re-establishing trust between our military and civilian communities. Even then there's no guarantee. You've exceeded your authority."

At first, he thinks his words may actually have had an effect. Wolff halts, his back still turned to him.

"Is that really what you want to do?" the German says over his shoulder. "Have you considered carefully?"

"Certainly."

But when Wolff turns around, Max sees no anxiety or concern in his features.

"Then you must go ahead, Monsieur. I am sure my superiors will be interested to hear from you. However, I doubt that it will change their decision."

"What decision? What are you suggesting? What decision has been made, Major?"

But just like last night, Wolff will not be drawn. "Dinon will find out in due course. I bid you good day."

He continues to his vehicle. The engine rumbles into life and he departs.

*　　*　　*

Max finds, without surprise, that the mairie has been searched. The scene is a familiar one by now—filing cabinets and cupboards emptied, their contents thrown everywhere, desks and chairs upended.

What with this and the hideous poster on the wall outside, Hortense is almost speechless with anger. But only almost.

"I'd take a gun to Wolff myself if I had one. Do we have any guns, Max?"

"Please behave, Hortense. Your arrest would be a great nuisance to me."

He straightens the furniture and helps her gather the scattered papers and files together, then leaves her to sort them while he works on the letter to avenue Kléber, drafting and redrafting it in longhand until it is ready for typing. At least the typewriter has survived.

He knows the letter will not be heeded. He knows he has no chance of obtaining financial restitution. He knows Wolff will not be taken to task by his superiors in Paris. The exact opposite is more likely.

But these considerations do not matter. They are not the point. He writes the letter because it is what any other civic leader would do. And that is how he must always behave and appear: as an ordinary civic leader; no more, no less. That is the point of the letter.

Wolff's taunt echoes in his head as he signs the letter and returns it to Hortense for despatch by messenger.

"Dinon will find out in due course."

Though he wishes otherwise, his prediction to Pierre is being fulfilled. This will be the something else about which he speculated. Exactly what it will be, he still does not know—but it is sure to involve reprisals of some kind. Military High Command has already made its decision. The poster featuring Jean-Luc threatens punishment for any individual withholding information, but Wolff's remark implies punishment on a wider scale—collective punishment of the town: arrests, imprisonment, perhaps worse.

Precisely what Max told Sophie could happen. Precisely what he and the people of Dinon have always worked so hard to avoid.

CHAPTER 14

"WE MUST DO everything we can to get along with the Germans."

From the day of Egon Wolff's arrival, this is what Max has told the people of Dinon, whether in meetings of the Dinon town council or in the streets and markets where he walks with and speaks to his citizens.

"We must survive—that's our duty, survival. Not to oppose them but to survive."

It has never been easy. Week by week the food shortages have grown worse. Ration allowances are reduced without warning and even then are rarely fulfilled. People stand patiently in line for coupons that turn out to be worthless because there is nothing for which to exchange them.

Yet there is never any shortage of rules, constraints or humiliations for the people of Dinon. These began with the curfew and the blackout.

"These measures will protect your citizens," Wolff tried to assure Max. "A curfew keeps trouble off the streets. It will make criminal activity more difficult. Your police chief agrees."

"Jacques Dompnier will agree to anything that gives him and his bullies an excuse to push people around. A blackout will make crime easier, no matter what he says."

"You see it wrongly. Are you doing this on purpose? The curfew and blackout will hinder the movement of black-market goods."

"There'd be no black market if your Reich wasn't stripping France bare."

German military and civilian personnel and those engaged by the Reich take priority over ordinary citizens in shops, bars, cafés, restaurants and other public premises. These priority customers are not to be made stand in line but have to be served at once.

The Germans watch films featuring their favorite stars in the plush comfort of their own Soldatenkino. They enjoy seemingly endless supplies of cigarettes and chocolate. They consume cakes and sip coffee in their Soldatenkaffee while the people of Dinon scour the streets for scraps.

The Germans are looters. Common thieves. The Reich shows them the way by making France pay the cost of her own occupation. No surprise, then, that ordinary soldiers follow suit. They help themselves to anything that takes their fancy. Rugs are rolled up and taken to the barracks, to make the officers' mess more homely. Comfortable armchairs go the same way. Curtains are torn from windows and carted away.

When Max protests, as he does regularly, Wolff's eyes glaze over.

"Unfortunate circumstances befall everyone in wartime, Monsieur. We must all expect a degree of dislocation of our normal life. Tell your citizens that."

*   *   *

Christmas was the worst time.

Only the Germans had a Christmas tree. Only the Germans had a party—in the barracks, though the people of Dinon heard their laughter, could not help but smell the maddening aromas of their food, and saw them stagger about drunkenly.

The Germans attended their own religious services and sang their own hymns. They crooned sentimental songs in the Soldatenkaffe. Strapping louts ready enough to swing a fist or a rifle butt into a Dinon face grew maudlin and longed for home.

Wolff issued a special Christmas edition of *La Voix de Dinon*, with colorful illustrations of snowy German landscapes and happy German families gathered around cozy firesides and tables laden with food.

"It shows how good life is in the Fatherland," he told Max. "A good place to live, a good place to work. These benefits are what the Reich will bring the people of France—and the people of Dinon."

"You think so?" thundered Max in fury at the German's stupidity. "When will these benefits begin?"

As for the people of Dinon, they had letters to write and gifts to send off to their menfolk who were still in German prison camps or had been compelled to work in German industry. The gifts were simple, all that could be managed, each of them an act of self-denial and personal sacrifice on the sender's part: a pair of thick wool socks, a cake of soap.

There was no way of knowing whether the parcels and mail ever got through or were lost or stolen. Max tried to find out but it was a waste of time. Wolff was no help.

"The Reich has other priorities," he said, and went back to his paperwork.

A few postcards arrived from the prisoners and forced workers, their content restricted to a maximum of seven lines of text. Few of the writers accomplished even that much. The busy German censors, as sharp eyed as that Nazi eagle, made sure there was never anything negative, no criticisms, no complaints, in their content.

Only bland platitudes that told the addressees nothing about how their loved ones were really faring.

"We're looking forward to the two days of rest we've been promised."

"I send you a big kiss and my very best wishes for the new year."

In the weeks leading to the festive season Max and Bruno skimmed as much as they could from the Picardie's rations to share with the most needy of the town; it was pitifully little, for the Ministry of Provisions watched every bag of flour, every pinch of sugar, every sausage.

As Christmas finally arrived, the people of Dinon made the best of things, like their Savior in his straw-lined manger in the Nativity scene in Père Bastien's church. The blessings of Christmas would be meager but they were the more precious for existing at all: home-made toys for the children; new clothes fashioned from old; an extra pat of butter on the table, saved specially for the festive occasion; a coin to bring a child good fortune in the coming year.

Wolff spent Christmas at the barracks with his men. Max and Bruno dined on a few leftovers in the bar of the Picardie. They raised their glasses.

"To survival."

This was Dinon's Christmas.

CHAPTER 15

SHE IS EXHAUSTED but she cannot sleep. She lies on the bed—*his* bed—and tries to rest, aware that she must restore her strength. The shaving mirror reflects the daylight outside this prison where he has locked her away; she watches the oval of light as it travels across the wall.

So the German she shot is dead. Yet she feels no sense of satisfaction, takes no pleasure in justice having been done for Gérard and her parents. There is only this dull ache because she has taken a human life. A German life, yes, but still a life. She never thought she would feel this way.

It angers her, this unexpected sense of remorse. It eats at her, a dark weight of guilt—for guilt is what it is, and guilt, she knows, is merely self-indulgence. Her imprisonment, that is where she should be directing her attention, to that and to what Max Duval, the vile collaborator, has in mind for her. For it is exactly as she said: he is waiting for the right moment, then he will hand her over to his Feldkommandant and collect his thirty pieces of silver. She must not let that happen.

She plucks at the clothes she is wearing—*his* clothes. She despises him yet she has wrapped her body in garments that have known his body. But it was a purely practical choice, she tells herself; there was nothing else for her to wear.

At another time there could have been other clothing for her, however, female clothing, because at some other time a woman used this bedroom. She can tell because of the smell—perfume, faded and faint, like a memory almost forgotten, but still here, in the bedding, the walls, the few sticks of furniture. She has been conscious of it ever since she entered the room.

And then there is the old oak wardrobe. It takes little imagination to guess that its bare rails and empty drawers once carried female garments.

So who was—or is—this vanished woman? A wife? A lover? Did she live alone in this room or did she share the room and the bed with Max? What has become of her? Nothing of her is left, there are no feminine items in the bathroom. As if she has gone forever. That wardrobe cleared so assiduously of every stitch of female clothing. Nothing overlooked, nothing left behind.

She remembers how Max busied himself at the bedside table when he brought her here, blocking her view of what he was doing.

What *was* he doing?

She rises from the bed and begins to search.

And finds the framed photographs behind the wardrobe. Clumsily hidden because that was all he could manage in those hasty moments.

*   *   *

She is hungry. She lifts the lid of the coffee pot. The coffee is cold. The croissants are as dry as paper.

The words embroidered on the napkin catch her eye. *Hôtel Picardie*. For a second time she pushes the tray away, vowing that nothing from his Hôtel Picardie will pass her lips. But she wets a fingertip, dips it in the sugar and puts it to her tongue. She cannot remember the last time she tasted sugar. She groans at the sweetness.

On the wall the oval of daylight moves on.

*   *   *

Footsteps are approaching. She jumps to her feet, readies herself for another argument, another lecture.

A key turns; the door opens.

But the person standing there is not Max. It is a giant of a man who seems to her startled gaze to be almost as tall and as broad as the doorway. He is wearing a chef's white jacket and trousers, and is carrying a tray on which there is a covered serving dish. A murderous-looking meat cleaver hangs at his waist. His expression is sour behind his bushy moustache.

"So you're the cause of all the fuss," he growls. "You're Sophie." He almost spits the name. "I won't say I'm pleased to make your acquaintance."

"Who are you? Another collaborator?"

"I'm Bruno. And you should watch your mouth."

He puts his tray down and picks up the one with the untouched coffee and croissants.

"No appetite? Well, it's fine by me if you leave this as well." Meaning the contents of the serving dish. "Starve yourself to death if you like. We don't want you here. You weren't invited and you wouldn't be missed, God knows."

"Nobody wants me here but nobody will let me go. Max made that clear enough."

"I'm not like Max. I'd let you go. I'd toss you to the Boche like I'd chuck a bone to a pack of hounds." He eyes her disparagingly. "A bone with not much meat."

His gaze on her body makes her shudder.

"You're a student, I suppose."

"Why do you suppose that?"

"You're the type—know-it-all. The type that knows everything and knows nothing."

"Here's something I know. There are people in Paris who'll deal with collaborators like you once we've got rid of the Germans."

"Paris?" he echoes. "Paris!"

He crowds in on her, pressing his free hand to the wall so that she is trapped. The fist is huge; he could throttle her with just that one hand. Or dismember her with the cleaver. She smells stale tobacco on his breath. Somehow she manages to hold her ground, does not turn away or lower her eyes but glares defiantly up at him.

"Paris has nothing to do with us here," he growls. "And we want nothing to do with Paris. What we do here is our business, not theirs. Get that lesson into your skull. Yap as much as you like about collaborators, but just don't cause us any problems while you're here."

He withdraws his hand but only in order to smack the wall with its palm. She feels the breeze as the hand skims past her head. The sound of the blow is like an explosion in the confined space of the room.

Then he steps back, turns and is gone. The key scrapes in the lock, his footsteps recede.

Her legs fold beneath her, her strength drained by the confrontation. She slumps on the bed, more certain than ever of her need to get away from here.

Her gaze finds the covered serving dish.

CHAPTER 16

BY THE TIME Max cycles away from the mairie, Wolff's poster of Jean-Luc is everywhere, the young man's face with its dead eyes staring out from every stretch of wall, street corner and gable end that Max passes.

In the warehouse district, as elsewhere, the military presence has been stepped up. Some patrolling troopers are watching as he enters Auguste's yard. But he takes care not to meet their gaze and they do not trouble him.

Yesterday when he called on Auguste the premises were more or less orderly, if crammed. Today they look as if a whirlwind has hit. Countless numbers of small pieces of metal type, each one an individual alphabet letter or print character, litter the ground. Shattered bits of printing equipment and rolls of blank newsprint, all destroyed, clutter the doorway of the print room. Boxes of stationery have been burst open and emptied. The galley proofs of *La Voix de Dinon* are torn and scattered across the yard. There will be no edition of the newspaper this week—or possibly for many weeks. At least that loss will be Wolff's alone; it will certainly not be Dinon's.

Max stows the bicycle behind a large bin and goes in search of Auguste. Tiny pieces of type bite into the soles of his boots.

As he enters the long print room with its great press, Auguste comes shuffling into view at the other end, moving distractedly through the debris, a wooden tray of type in his arms. His gaze is fixed on the floor, as if he is trying to make a tally of the endless tiny pieces down there. He crouches down and begins collecting them into the tray. He is sniffling and seems to be on the brink of tears. He does not notice Max.

"You printed that poster, Auguste. The one with the dead boy."

Auguste looks up, taken by surprise. He rises to his feet with a heavy sigh. He passes an ink-stained hand over his eyes. Max wonders if he is wiping away a tear.

"More than that, my dear Max—I took the photograph as well, may God forgive me."

"How could you do such a thing?"

Auguste leads him into the shadows beyond the press, out of hearing should any troopers enter the yard.

"At gunpoint, that's how, with Wolff standing over me." He gestures vaguely at the wreckage surrounding him. "This is how his thugs rewarded me afterwards. My house is as bad. You know how ill my Marie is—you can imagine what it's done to her."

Max knows he will be adding to Auguste's troubles but he has no choice; besides, Auguste has brought it upon himself.

"Stay here," he tells the printer.

He fetches the bicycle, wheels it into the print room and props it against the press.

"This is yours, I believe. True commitment to the cause, that you were prepared to sacrifice it so generously."

There is a flicker of recognition in Auguste's eyes at the sight of the machine.

"I don't know what you mean, Max. What cause?"

"Communism."

"Is this one of Pierre's stupid jokes?"

"It's not a joke, Auguste. I couldn't be more serious."

Auguste looks nervously from the bicycle to Max, and back to the bicycle. Max knows how his mind will be working. Claim the bicycle and there is no telling what Max may be planning for him. But disown the valuable machine and he forfeits any chance of ever getting it back.

A hopeful light comes to his eyes.

"Yes, it's mine—but it was stolen."

Max shakes his head, dismissing the lie. "And the other bicycle? Do you want me to believe that one was stolen too?"

"What other bicycle?"

"Two gunmen, two bicycles. They each had one, and I'm saying you supplied both. Probably also a map and detailed directions. So the killings were possible only because of you. What happened last night and what Wolff is putting Dinon through now—it's all down to you, Auguste."

The little printer is beginning to grasp that more is at stake than the loss or return of a bicycle or two.

"You avoided being shot by Wolff this morning," Max continues. "But you know I should shoot you right now, don't you? If Bruno was here, he'd already have pulled the trigger."

"For God's sake, Max!"

The tray of type begins to shake, the tiny pieces of metal rattling against their wooden enclosure. Max takes the tray from Auguste's quivering hands and places it on a nearby table. Auguste stares longingly at it as though he regrets its absence. Now tears are definitely glistening in his eyes.

"Auguste, I'm giving you this one chance. The Dinon cell needs you. We depend on your skill and technical expertise. Your work is the very best."

A loud sniffle. "I know all that."

"But now it's time for you to choose—you can work with us or you can work with your communist friends. You can't work with both. Not any longer. That's over now. Cast your lot with your communist comrades and I can't promise you safety—you know too much. The cell will have to vote on what should be done about you. Even if you get through that, who knows what Bruno might take it into his head to do?"

"Wait, Max. Let's have no more talk of shooting. And for God's sake keep Bruno out of it. All right, so maybe I did help certain comrades. But don't you think it's time for direct action—patriotic action? That's what they believe in, the comrades."

"Is that what you call last night—patriotic action? Will it drive the Germans out of Dinon? Will it liberate France one day sooner? All it does is make our work in the cell harder and more dangerous. Do you think Wolff will let it pass? What he's doing now is only the start. There'll be worse to come. You've stirred up a hornets' nest. You've been a fool."

Auguste is shaking his head, not in denial of the accusation but because he has heard all he needs of the case against him.

"What do you want from me, Max?"

"Only what we always agreed, no more than that, but also no less—to keep on using your skill and expertise, and to know you'll stay away from your communist comrades. The work our cell does is more important than their antics. And there's the problem of their security."

"What about it?"

"It's not good enough. That's more danger for you—and therefore for the Dinon cell as well if you're captured and interrogated. So that's it, Auguste. It's time for you to make your choice once and for all—it's us or the comrades. Who's it going to be?"

Auguste moves to retrieve the wooden tray. Max reaches out and stops him. Auguste settles for running his inky fingers over the small metal pieces. They seem to comfort him. They click as he presses them into place.

"Maybe I made some poor decisions. Maybe I can see that now. But I didn't know when the attack on Wolff's men would happen, I didn't know that, Max, I promise you—I didn't know it would interfere with our plans."

"You should have thought of that."

"Maybe, maybe. I would never want to jeopardize the cell's work."

"You say that, yet here we are. So where do we go from here? Where do *you* go?"

Auguste takes a deep breath, releases it. "Very well, then. You know what I choose. I'll have no more to do with the comrades."

Max looks closely at him, searching for the truth. As with the others in the cell, he counts Auguste as a friend, a true friend. They have known each other since they were children. Bruno too. Always it was the three of them, always together, always looking out for one another. All the way into adulthood, always there for each other in good times and bad. Side by side in that other war. The little printer shouldered Geneviève's coffin along with Bruno and Pierre and Max himself. These bonds last; they count for something.

Now Max too has a decision to make. Perhaps in his heart he has made it already; all it needed was Auguste's contrition.

He will continue to trust him.

"What about your equipment and materials? Have you still got what you need?"

Auguste looks relieved at this welcome return to normal considerations.

"My camera is safe, thanks to Wolff—what an irony—and I have supplies of everything else, all well hidden. These German gorillas aren't that bright." He thinks for a moment and looks up at Max, a glint in his eye. "Just tell me this, dear Max—how did you end up with the bicycle anyway?"

"I found it."

Auguste risks a wary grin. "Found it? Very well, whatever you say. And how did you know it was used by one of the gunmen?"

"Just a lucky guess."

"Ah, I see. Right."

"And now no more of your questions, Auguste."

"What makes you think the comrades' security is no good?"

"You'll just have to take my word."

"The gunman who got away—any sign of him?"

"None. I said that's enough, Auguste. No more questions."

"An old newshound's habit. Just one last question, then—so the gunman has disappeared?"

"No trace of him anywhere."

This pleases the printer. "Do you think he can escape? Do you think he might even be gone from here already?"

"Why concern yourself?"

"Humor me, dear Max."

Max considers. "In my opinion, Wolff won't find the man he's looking for. But that's only my opinion."

He pushes the bicycle away from the press and passes it to Auguste. It is time to return to the Picardie. On foot.

*   *   *

On the way back he faces the nuisance of the roadblocks again. As he anticipated earlier, the troopers and their canine companions are aggressive and on edge from their long spell in the sun. At each roadblock the men shout hoarsely at him when he comes into view, and press the business end of their rifles against his chest. The dogs bare their teeth and snarl.

Each time the same stupid performance. Each time the same mindless questions. But unlike this morning, he is hardly aware of the troopers' nonsense. He shows his identity card and answers their questions, but his mind is elsewhere.

Auguste behaved foolishly. But what if that is not the end of the danger? What if his is not the only folly? What if Max's protection of Sophie Carrière is as dangerous to the cell as anything Auguste has done?

What then?

For the third time today, he questions the wisdom of his actions. For the third time he wonders what kind of mistake he may be making.

CHAPTER 17

GENEVIÈVE.

Never far from his mind, never far away, and now, following the confrontation with Auguste and the remembrance of her funeral, very much in the forefront of his thoughts.

He will be checking table settings in the dining room and will look up to find her seated at a table, smiling as she watches him. He can stand beneath the plane trees in front of the Picardie and hear her voice in the whisper of the leaves. He hears her laughter when the notes of the evening Angelus bell in Père Bastien's little church drift out to the Picardie. The little church she loved. But with no place in its graveyard for her. The old priest denied her that. That man of tradition. Too much tradition. Unbending tradition and little Christian love.

Her clothes are gone from the bedroom—where Sophie now trespasses—but Max is certain that something of her still remains there. He wonders if Sophie senses her presence. He wonders if that is possible.

Recently there have been times when he cannot see Geneviève's face properly, times when he cannot recall her walk or her hands or how she raised a wine glass or how she would move beside him in the quiet of an evening. The touch of her hand, the softness of her cheek—these he cannot bring to mind. There are whole days when her smile or her voice eludes him. He loses the music of her laughter.

Her bicycle still stands beside his in the barn, just as he told Egon Wolff. But sometimes when he sets off for Dinon, a journey they made together almost every day, he is unable to picture her ahead of him on rue de la République. There is only the black, deserted road. Empty. He cycles alone.

They pass, these periods of blankness, but that they arise at all disturbs him. He fears that Geneviève is fading from his memory, that he is guilty of allowing this to happen.

And the prospect of losing her all over again terrifies him.

CHAPTER 18

AT THE PICARDIE he finds Bruno in his kitchen. By now it is looking more or less as it should.

"I sent Paul home," explains the chef. "Better for him not to be here while we have your angry young friend as company. Virginie finished her shift and she's gone."

"*My* young friend?"

"Well, she's sure as hell no friend of mine."

Max tells him about Auguste.

"He always was a damned fool," is Bruno's verdict. "You should have shot him."

"I've dealt with the matter. He won't stray again."

"You'd better be right."

"So how is our unexpected guest?"

Bruno scowls and lights a cigarette. "Unexpected and unwanted. She calls us collaborators. She's restless, as jittery as a flea. The risk is, she'll make a run for it and get caught. That'll be the end of us, Max, and the end of the cell. It's insane having her here. The sooner we get rid of her the better. And if we can't do it any other way, we should put a bullet in the back of her head."

"We won't do that."

"Then what's your plan—what do we do with her?"

"She has to stay here until the Germans calm down."

"That's not answering my question. Besides, do you honestly think Wolff will calm down?"

Max tells him about the Feldkommandant's poster seeking information about Sophie and her dead accomplice.

The chef snorts ruefully. "So now any imbecile with a grudge against you or me can claim there's something going on here at the Picardie. If Wolff raids us again, this time he won't end up empty handed."

"He won't search the Picardie again."

"Why not?"

"Because he's working on something else. I think avenue Kléber has made a decision over his head. He refuses to say what it is, but I don't think it'll be more searches."

"Something worse, then. We've gone beyond searches, you think?"

"Possibly."

"Well, we'll find out soon enough. And I'll tell you this—whatever it is, we should be worried."

Max cannot argue with that.

*　　*　　*

He looks in on Sophie. She seems to be walking back and forth in the small bedroom and has to stop for lack of floor space when he arrives. She stands with her back to the window, crosses her arms and glares at him.

"You've made a prisoner of me. Look how you lock me in. Why not hand me over to your Germans right now? Get it over with. Go ahead."

"I lock the door to keep others out. You should be grateful to be here—if you were in the hands of the man who's hunting you, how long would it be before you'd tell him everything about your operations in Paris?"

"That would never happen."

"Wouldn't it? Judging from what I've seen so far of your leaders' incompetence, my guess is they've allowed you to know far more than you should—identities of cell members, meeting places, names of sympathizers, planned actions. Am I right?"

A silent glare.

"In other words, more than is safe for any one person to know. You'd give the Germans everything. You wouldn't last an hour under interrogation."

That angers her.

"Even if you're right about what I know—"

"And I am."

"I'd tell the Germans nothing."

"You'd be a gold mine."

He picks up the tray to leave and raises the cover of the serving dish. At least she has had the sense to eat.

"I've been arrested before," she is saying. "Arrest doesn't frighten me."

He stops at the door and turns back to her. "What did you say? Why were you arrested?"

A shadow passes across her face. Has she let slip an unintended admission?

"It was because of something my brother did. Our family was taken in for questioning by the Paris police. Being Jewish didn't help. Yes, I'm a Jew. Not much of one, but a Jew is a Jew. In those days, at the start of the occupation, my father and mother still had influential friends—they helped to get us released."

"Then you were lucky."

"Since when is it lucky to be Jewish?"

"Arrest by the police for a civil crime is one thing, capture in connection with a terrorist offence against the Reich is another thing entirely. There'll be no influential friends capable of bailing you out if you're captured for that. Tell me, what was your brother's offence?"

But apparently the conversation has gone as far as she will allow. She pushes her hair aside and gives him her familiar glare again. "Why should any of this matter to a collaborator?"

"Whatever your brother did, I can tell you that your experience of arrest and questioning by the police—even as a Jew—bears no resemblance to how you'll be treated by the Germans if they capture you. Our Feldkommandant is a determined man, he won't give up his hunt for you, and if he finds you he'll extract everything he wants from you, believe me."

She continues giving him that black look without making any reply.

He leaves.

*   *   *

Parisian Jews. So is this her loss: both parents and a brother? What became of them? What was her brother's crime?

He returns to the kitchen. Bruno looks up from the steel counter he is scouring.

"Did you know our young Paul has found himself a girlfriend?"

Max is glad of the distraction. "Paul Burnand, the shyest boy in Dinon? I didn't know. Who's the lucky girl?"

"That's where things get slightly complicated. It's Yvette Dompnier—Jacques Dompnier's daughter."

"Ah. Complicated indeed."

There is no one in Dinon with as high an opinion of himself as the police chief. His plans for the Dompnier bloodline are unlikely to include his daughter falling for a simple working lad like Paul Burnand.

"Does Dompnier know?"

"According to Paul, no. But it won't take long for it to come out. Dompnier will explode. He beats his wife. I dread to think what he might do to Yvette. It's a dangerous business, this falling in love."

Something else with which Max cannot argue.

CHAPTER 19

SHE HAD TRIED with all her might to open the window, but the hinges and crank were rusted solid. She considered smashing the glass pane, but the noise might have been heard, bringing someone to investigate. At worst the Germans themselves might have come snooping if they were in the hotel.

Of all unlikely helpers, it was the chef, the great oaf called Bruno, who came to her rescue. She appreciated the meal he brought her, even though he so clearly begrudged her every mouthful. She was ravenous, and when she lifted the lid from the serving dish, the sight and aroma of the food, medallions of steak, overpowered her. She set her principles aside and devoured the lot.

So she did appreciate the food. But she appreciated the cutlery even more. Once she had cleared the plate, she got to work with the knife on the ancient putty of the casement, gathering the debris into the napkin to conceal it. It was what she was doing when she heard Max approach.

But the foolish man saw nothing, noticed nothing—not even the fact that the knife was missing from the tray. He was too busy being pompous.

She resumed her digging as soon as he had gone. And kept on digging even when the tears came. Tears caused by the memories she had stirred up.

She puts the knife down now, wipes her eyes on her sleeve and rests her aching hands.

She regrets telling him so much. Her family and what happened to them are her concern and hers alone. But her guard was down and she had a moment of weakness. Entirely her own fault. She should never have mentioned the arrest. But suddenly she wanted to talk, and the recognition of that need frightens her now. She wanted to let the story pour out as if she was a silly child looking for solace.

Solace? From *him*?

That was not all. She wanted to ask him about the woman in the photographs, the woman who wore the clothes that are no longer here but whose perfume still haunts the room. She wanted to hear his story and wanted to tell her own. As if the two of them could talk like normal strangers.

What has happened to her? Where have these feelings come from, what has caused them? Why should she want to tell this man anything—this collaborator—or hear anything about him in return? Why should she care about the woman in the photographs?

Somehow she managed to halt her flow of words before it became a torrent. She did not ask about the woman; at least she can give herself credit for that. She held his gaze to the very end, eye to eye, while he stood there. She knew that if she weakened, if she looked away, the tears would come.

She willed him to leave her in peace and solitude.

And hated it when he did.

CHAPTER 20

IT IS LATE when Wolff returns to the Picardie. He and the aide consume the remainder of Bruno's steak medallions.

"Well, Monsieur Duval, have you sent your letter of complaint to Military High Command?"

"I have."

"Very good." Wolff dabs his lips. "We will talk tomorrow. We will meet formally, as Feldkommandant and mayor."

"What's there to talk about? Avenue Kléber won't have replied. With all respect, I'd like to hear from them first."

"Monsieur, with all respect in return, what you would like is not my concern. Nor avenue Kléber's. You and I will meet tomorrow morning. Formally."

* * *

Max clears up in the dining room and helps Bruno with his final chores in the kitchen.

Again, Bruno is willing to stay overnight.

"Not necessary," says Max.

"They might come tonight."

"And they might equally well not. Or any night. They might be sent back up the line and on to a different cell, a different route, a safer one. Go home and sort your house out. Have you forgotten?"

"Bastards," mutters Bruno, reminded of what still awaits him at home as a result of Wolff's search operation.

He bundles his whites into the laundry and departs.

*　*　*

After a while Max goes to the end of the ground-floor corridor that leads to Bruno's kitchen. Here, in this corner, is where the veins and arteries of the Picardie converge and cross one another. These are the pipes of the plumbing system, running between the upstairs bathrooms and toilets, the boiler down in the basement and the sewage system. The pipes to which he is ever attentive.

Max knows every pipe and its purpose. He knows which ones transport hot water and which cold water to Wolff's suite and to the bathroom on the floor below him that his aide uses. He knows which pipes are the drainage pipes that discreetly carry away what must be carried away.

To his mind, they are a defining characteristic of civilization, these pipes. But these days they have become more than that; these days they help him and Bruno play the hand they have been dealt, just as Max said they should.

He waits patiently for all the familiar gurgling and trickling and wheezing to stop. Occasionally he touches a finger to a pipe that seems to have gone quiet, searching for a vibration in order to confirm whether it is still in use, much as Doctor Pierre might search for a pulse.

When all has been silent and without vibration for a time, he climbs the service stairs and moves along the corridors of the upper floors, pausing outside Wolff's suite and the aide's room to listen for any sounds of movement from within. In the same way as he knows the pipes of the plumbing so intimately, so he knows every stair tread and every floorboard—which ones creak and are to be avoided, and which are silent and can safely be stepped upon. He could move with eyes closed through every part of the Picardie and not misplace a step or create a sound.

When he is confident that sleep has borne the Germans away, he returns downstairs to the lobby and fetches an old soft cap, a workman's cap, that he keeps behind the reception desk. He folds it and slips it into a pocket, extinguishes all the lights except the dim bulb over the main staircase, and takes his place at the lobby's front windows, his back to Duc Henri.

He peels back an edge of one of the blackout blinds. The grounds outside are dark, a landscape of shadows that seem to shift and waver as his gaze passes over them. The sky is solidly overcast to the horizon. No break in the clouds, no moonlight seeping through, no stars visible.

A perfect night, therefore.

It might be tonight after all.

Nothing more for him and Duc Henri to do now but wait.

CHAPTER 21

"Monsieur Max," said Virginie the housekeeper one day, "there are no photographs in that Major Wolff's rooms. Not a single photograph anywhere."

"Is that a problem?"

"No evidence of a wife or girlfriend."

"Not our business, Virginie."

"No photographs of children. No mother or father. No one, not even a dog if he has one back in Germany. Why is that? Isn't there anyone he misses? Does he have anyone to miss? Or anyone who misses him?"

"Virginie—"

"All there is in his suite is a big photograph of that Hitler. His aide has one as well. Do all Germans have him on their walls? Those salutes they do. They worship him."

"Virginie."

"Monsieur Max?"

"These matters are no concern of ours. Major Wolff is a guest of the Picardie. Clean his suite each day, collect and return his laundry, change his bed linen. Exactly as with any other guest in the old days. Our circumstances have changed but our standards have not."

She looked daggers at him but said no more.

*   *   *

Once a week Max enters Wolff's suite when the German is absent. He assesses the condition of the furniture and soft furnishings, checks that windows and doors function smoothly, runs the bath taps and shower head, tests the flush of the toilet and passes his finger over surfaces in search of dust. He visits the aide's room as well and the bathroom on that floor, and gives them similar attention. From the outset he advised Wolff that he would perform these checks.

"This is my responsibility as your host, Major. I do the same in all the rooms when they have guests. An essential duty."

"We all have our duties, Monsieur Duval."

Max finds that Virginie was right: there are no photographs other than the one of Hitler.

It is as if Egon Wolff has sprung from nowhere and exists only to serve the German Reich and war.

*   *   *

But Egon Wolff has not sprung from nowhere.

Max remembers a miserable, wet Sunday when it rained without pause from before dawn. The mairie being closed on that day of rest, he had remained in the Picardie.

In the middle of the afternoon, Wolff returned from Dinon with two briefcases packed with papers. Max watched him stride past, the aide following with two more hefty briefcases. It had happened before—days when Wolff sequestered himself in his suite to catch up with paperwork. His Reich seemed to float on bureaucracy and paper.

"I am not to be disturbed," he commanded as he headed for the staircase and his suite.

But an hour or so later a motorcycle messenger arrived, demanding to see him. The messenger was soaking wet. His boots were filthy with mud, water streamed from his leathers and greatcoat, gathering in a dirty puddle at his feet. He had obviously been riding for some hours—not a messenger from the garrison, then, but most likely all the way from Paris, from avenue Kléber. That made him someone Wolff would want to receive, regardless of his earlier command.

Sure enough, the Feldkommandant appeared on the staircase, having heard the motorcycle approach. He was as formally attired in full uniform as if he had been working in the Kommandantur rather than in the privacy of his suite.

Max left the two men to it and went to the bar—to be exact, he went to the particular spot at the end of the counter, where he could observe them in the mirror without risk of being seen. He picked up an already clean and dry glass and busied himself polishing it further while his gaze remained on the mirror.

The messenger removed his gauntlets, snapped open a leather-bound notebook and held it out for Wolff to sign. That done, he handed the Feldkommandant a leather pouch, the kind used by the Germans for carrying documents and correspondence. Wolff turned his back and took a few steps away for privacy, opened the pouch and withdrew an envelope, evidently the only contents. This he stared at for some moments, as though reluctant to open it. At last he did so.

Either the single sheet of paper within told him nothing of interest or its message was very brief, for he looked at it for no more than five or six seconds before folding it back into its envelope and putting it into an inside pocket of his tunic. He stood there for a minute or so, ramrod straight, then turned briskly back to the messenger, said something to him and returned the now empty pouch. They saluted; the messenger departed.

Max moved away from the corner. He listened to Wolff's footsteps, muffled on carpets or echoing on the wooden flooring. They went first to the library, then the dining room, until finally Wolff arrived at the bar, though he came only as far as the doorway.

Max continued polishing the glass.

Wolff cleared his throat. "You have cognac?"

Max looked up as though only now registering his presence. "Yes, Major. We have cognac."

"You will send a bottle and a glass to my room. I will not require dinner this evening."

*   *   *

It was after one o'clock in the morning when Max heard Wolff descend the stairs. He himself remained where he was, out of sight in the deep shadows of the lobby. Wolff's progress was slow but steady, the delicate, considered progress of a man who knew he was beyond the edge of sobriety but had not forgone self-discipline. He let himself out to the courtyard. Max heard the sound of the bottle clinking against the door as he drew it closed after him.

The rain continued to hammer down.

It was almost four o'clock when the Feldkommandant returned. The sound of his movements was very different now: stumbling, uncertain.

Max came forward just in time to catch him when he missed his footing on the staircase.

"Steady, Major."

He raised him up. There was no sign of the bottle of cognac. The rain had not eased, and Wolff was soaked through. He stank of alcohol.

He squinted at Max in the dim lighting.

"Monsieur Duval." The words were slurred.

Max glimpsed something white by the German's feet on the stairs. A piece of folded paper. It was the envelope that the messenger had brought. The single sheet poked out from a corner. When Max was sure that Wolff had regained his balance, he bent down and picked up the envelope. It was sodden and limp.

Wolff took it from him immediately. He was not too drunk for that. He spoke again as he pressed the envelope safely away into a pocket.

"My brother."

He mumbled something in German, nothing that Max could understand, then seemed to search for some thought—an idea, a word in French perhaps—that was eluding him. Finally he seemed to find it. He tilted his head to focus on Max. The scar on his face was white in the gloom.

"My late brother."

* * *

Two hours later he was up and about at his customary hour. He was pale and the whiff of alcohol still hung on his breath, but he managed some breakfast, then his aide took him and his briefcases off to Dinon.

Neither Wolff nor Max ever mentioned the events of that cold, wet night.

And Max recounted them to no one, not even Bruno.

But he knew that Egon Wolff, loyal servant of the German Reich, had not sprung from nowhere.

CHAPTER 22

SHE IS IN shock. Her heart is pounding as if it is trying to burst from her chest.

As she was digging at the putty of the window, she heard in the distance the faint whine of a vehicle engine. She stopped work at once, switched off the dim bedroom light, stood motionless and silent by the window, and listened. The noise grew louder; the vehicle was definitely coming towards the Hôtel Picardie.

She moved away from the window, intending to stay well out of sight as Max had instructed. On that at least she was prepared to follow his advice.

Then suddenly the vehicle was there, in the courtyard. Its headlight beams, partially masked, were still bright enough to send a fragment of light flickering into the now unlit bedroom. Germans were arriving—but not in force; there was only that single vehicle. Which meant it had to be the Feldkommandant returning for the night.

With that realization the temptation became too much for her. She had to see this man who was hunting her, this Feldkommandant who held Max in such thrall and whom he considered so dangerous.

The play of light in the room suggested that the vehicle was still manoeuvring as it parked. She edged forward cautiously until she could bring it into view. One of the occupants had already stepped down from it and was crossing the courtyard. A high-ranking officer in full uniform. He turned towards her as he passed through the headlight beams.

Her breath caught in her throat. It was as much as she could do to remain silent. She drew her head sharply back from the window. There was a sudden snapping sound and her knuckles slammed painfully against the pane of glass. For a second time she suppressed a cry. In her tension she had been pressing the knife against the window frame with all her might. She put the injured knuckles to her mouth.

The German had gone from her view now, so she looked down to see what had happened. Even at such close quarters, in the darkness she could hardly see the knife. Then she realized there was no knife to see. All she was holding was the handle, because that was all that was left. It took her a moment to understand that the blade had snapped off.

Something close to panic gripped her—the same feeling that had seized her on the railway embankment. Her response was the same as then: to push on, to be busy, to work. She dropped the useless handle, searched for and picked up the unattached blade and turned it about until she found the best way to grasp it—although no way was good—and resumed her digging as though that harsh physical effort might calm the pounding of her heart.

Now the blade is cutting into her fingers almost as much as it cuts the putty. But still she digs on, switching the blade from hand to hand, working with blind determination, like an animal that knows nothing else but this one instinct that impels it. She is oblivious to the pain and the fresh wounds every time her knuckles collide with the casement hinges and handle, every time the blade cuts a new gash in the soft flesh of her fingers.

That German. The Feldkommandant. She has all the more reason now for getting out of this accursed place where the collaborator Max Duval has imprisoned her.

In that moment when the German turned towards her, in that splash of light she saw his face. Only for a second or two. But it was enough. She was not mistaken.

Her heart pounds. In her shock and the flood of emotions that grip her, she can barely draw breath into her lungs.

But she digs blindly on.

CHAPTER 23

IT IS TWO o'clock in the morning before Max's patience is rewarded. Off to the left-hand side of the Picardie's grounds, beyond the plane trees and the old maze, well away from the main gateway, there appears briefly a tiny flicker of light. It could be a firefly or simply another night-time illusion, like the way the shadows shift as if alive. But ten seconds later it happens again, in exactly the same place.

He now has one minute in which to respond. If he does not, he will have two more chances, two more times when the light will appear twice, at ten-second intervals. If there is still no response from him, the rendezvous will be aborted, either for good or to be attempted on another night, provided that is possible—and bearing in mind that tonight may already be a second attempt.

He has a box of matches ready. He switches off the bulb over the staircase and raises the blackout blind. He strikes a light and extinguishes it immediately, allowing it to flare into life but no more. He counts ten seconds and repeats the procedure.

He lowers the blind and hurries up the service stairs as silently as before, and listens outside the door of Wolff's suite; from there he descends one flight and listens at the aide's door. Both men are snoring.

He returns downstairs and detours to the bar to collect the Browning, puts on the workman's cap, goes out to the courtyard and stands in the archway, where he strikes and immediately extinguishes a third match.

Seconds later, over to his left, a figure emerges from the darkness, a single shadow detaching itself from that landscape of shadows. If he looks directly at it he misses it; he has to focus his gaze past it to catch it in the corner of his eye, another trick of the darkness with which he has become familiar.

The figure may have entered the grounds just now through a side gate, or perhaps it was already waiting within the grounds. It crosses the grassy stretch between the old maze and the trees and moves towards him, head bowed as it watches its footing where the undergrowth has encroached on what was once a lawn.

The figure is silent, not praying—at any rate, not praying aloud—and it is certainly not sobbing. But out here on a lonely night, especially if a soft wind is moving through the trees, an observer's imagination—if there should happen to be an observer, one given to heeding country legends—such an observer's imagination could add those features readily enough.

As the old-timers in the bar of the Picardie tell each other with a shiver, maybe Duc Henri's ghostly friar exists; maybe not. It is all very well for Max to ridicule such tales, but who really knows, who can say for sure?

But the memory of the unfortunate monk, or the notion of him at least, is honored by this shadowy apparition passing through the night; and by the many others that have preceded it on moonless nights under Max Duval's vigilant gaze.

Should anyone other than Duc Henri be watching.

CHAPTER 24

SOPHIE IS WATCHING.

It took forever but she finally won her battle with the window and removed the pane of glass. She climbed out and made for the barn. It was somewhere to hide, a place where she could think. She badly needed to do that.

She was still shaken, her heart was still racing, and the pain in her damaged hands was almost unbearable. But there was more than physical pain for her to deal with.

Until that moment when she saw the German her plan had been straightforward—to recover her bicycle and be on her way. She was unarmed, she had no identity card, no money, all thanks to Max, but none of that would stop her. She would board a train somewhere, clandestinely, she would find a way, and hope for the best. She would choose a station further from Dinon than Rue because the Germans would be looking for her there. She would just keep going until she found a station where she could hide nearby until passenger trains resumed running. Or she might happen upon another freight train.

It would take as long as it took—possibly more than what was left of this night, so she might have to lie low during daylight hours. If the bicycle gave out on her, she would steal another one or walk.

She would steal food if she could not go without. Anything to get away from here and return to the familiar streets of Paris.

That was her plan, such as it was. A simple outline, with many flaws and gaps, but still a plan, something with which to start, to see her on her way. But now that simple plan is no longer enough. Not now. With the sight of that German, everything has changed.

But as she reaches the shelter of the barn her thoughts are interrupted by the quiet creak of a door somewhere in the courtyard behind her, a sound so quiet that she almost misses it. But she does hear, and crouches down in time to see someone step into the courtyard and go to stand under the archway. A man in a cap. A man with a gun in his hand.

She crouches lower, fearful he will see her, for he is looking all around. She realizes it is Max himself. Then she recognizes the same guardedness in him as she is exercising, and understands that he is not looking for her or anyone else down here at ground level; he is making sure he is not visible from any of the upstairs windows overlooking the courtyard.

Even more puzzling is the odd business with the match that she then witnesses, how Max lights it and extinguishes it all at once.

She sees a flutter of movement off to the left and watches in astonishment as a dark figure, no more than a shadow, appears out of nowhere, out of that deep countryside darkness she mistrusts, and seems to float over what must once have been the fancy gardens of this place. The figure joins Max in the archway.

All this in complete silence—no greetings exchanged, not a word spoken.

Moments later she sees the flutter of movement repeated as the night condenses into another shadow and a second figure materializes. It follows its predecessor to Max and the archway.

Again, no greetings, no words uttered. A silent and secret choreography of the night, intended, she is sure, for no audience of any kind—least of all her.

She waits. Seconds later, a third figure, also hurrying to the archway; also in silence.

She continues waiting, but this time the darkness remains undisturbed.

Three soundless shadows, all now hidden under that archway. All of them men, she is sure. And young, she thinks, considering how briskly they moved as they negotiated the dark grounds.

All joining Max as if they are in his care.

In his care? In a collaborator's care? Then what does that make them—fellow collaborators? More traitors for her to report to her leaders in Paris?

All this activity—suspicious and surely illegal—while his German guests sleep peacefully above, including the German Feldkommandant. She tries to make sense of what she is seeing. What is Max up to, Max Duval this friend of Germans, what is he doing at this hour that he so clearly does not want those same Germans to know about? Exactly what is going on here?

The answer comes to her. And it fits perfectly, because it is precisely what she would expect of him.

The black market. Profiteering.

What she is observing must be a deal of some kind in progress, an illicit meeting or business transaction. She recalls what he said about the special status of this precious hotel of his. He has access to goods that are unavailable to law-abiding citizens who lack influence and connections—so why not sell some of those goods on the black market?

It all makes sense now.

Or does it? Something still nags at her, a warning that this explanation is too simple. Nothing about Max Duval and this place is simple. She thinks again about those three shadowy figures in the archway with Max—all of them male, all of them young, moving so swiftly through this darkness that she hates.

Suddenly she finds herself confronted by another explanation. But it is so outrageous that she denies it at once, instinctively rules it out. Or tries to. Because that explanation would contradict everything she has discovered about this Hôtel Picardie and its proprietor.

But still . . . could that be the very point of this place? A place of contradictions. Like Max himself.

The possibility is there and she cannot pretend otherwise. This Hôtel Picardie may not be what it seems.

Likewise Max Duval.

"Who are you, Max Duval? *What* are you?"

CHAPTER 25

MAX CASTS A final glance towards where the tiny bursts of light appeared. No way of telling whether someone is still over there, waiting, watching to see if anything goes wrong, or whether they have already departed, their role complete, their part of tonight's undertaking done.

He makes the men stand close against the deep side wall of the arch, a blind spot hidden from the upstairs windows. He quickly pats each man down to check for weapons. Too many escape lines have been infiltrated by German agents and informers, with operators like him paying with their lives.

If all follows the usual procedure, the men will be here in the Picardie for only a few nights. He does not know who passed the message to Pierre that they were about to arrive. Nor does he know who will then take them from Juliette Labarthe when it is time for her to lead them out of Dinon and on to the next stage of their journey. He is the cell leader but he does not want this information.

The cell consists of the three of them—Max, Pierre and Juliette—plus Bruno, Auguste, and the cell's radio operator. Only Max knows the identity of this last individual, radio operators always being particularly fiercely protected because of the rarity of their skills and the extreme danger they put themselves in: radio signals can be monitored and tracked to source.

The radio operator is in fact Laure Rioche—none other than Widow Rioche, eavesdropper and apparent gossip. Her radio transmitter could have no better hiding place than within the complex wiring and delicate electronics of her switchboard.

Pierre's medical expertise and Juliette's pharmaceutical knowledge and stockroom of medical supplies complete the structure of a self-contained cell.

Always the priority is to protect the security of the escape line. So the Dinon cell is a cut-out from the rest of the line. And there are cut-outs within the cell itself: knowledge is restricted. Max is the only person who has to be in contact with Laure Rioche, which is why only he knows her identity. She in turn knows only of Max's involvement in their work; she does not know the identities or roles of the others.

All of them accept that if any of them is uncovered and interrogated by the Germans, they will inevitably give up everything they know—a simple reality. So the requirement is to limit the damage. What the individual does not know, they cannot tell. The rest of the line will remain secure, and Dinon's part in it can be rebuilt somewhere else. "Need to know only" is the golden rule, and they stick to it. The precautions they take are basic but they have served the cell and the escape line well.

It occurs to Max that Sophie Carrière's leaders, the hard men in Paris, could learn from the Dinon cell. Maybe one day they will.

But only if they last long enough.

CHAPTER 26

SHE HAS HEARD talk in Paris about secret underground networks that spirit people away from the Germans, conveying them along secret routes and through a system of safe houses and trusted contacts, links in chains that stretch the length of France and beyond. She has heard that these networks take people into Switzerland or over the Pyrenees to Spain, even across the Mediterranean from Marseille to North Africa, delivering them ultimately to safety in England.

Escape lines, she has heard them called. Is that what she is witnessing here tonight? Mysterious lights in dead of night; men flitting like ghosts through the darkness, allowing themselves to be searched as though they expect nothing less: not at all the behavior of equals in a business transaction, not even if it is a black-market trade.

Not the black market, then, but something even more illegal. And more dangerous. A form of resistance as hazardous as her own. Perhaps what appears to be a den of collaborators is the ideal cover for such an operation.

She remembers how Max criticized her leaders in Paris for sending her and Jean-Luc on their mission to Dinon. He claimed that such missions were a waste of life.

"There are other ways," was what he said.

What she is witnessing now—is this what he meant by those other ways? An escape line operating in the Hôtel Picardie?

If so, what does that do to her opinion of Max Duval?

CHAPTER 27

MAX STAYS BEHIND the men, the Browning semi-automatic
always in hand, and guides them in single file along the edge of the
courtyard, keeping close to the wall, and towards the rear service
door. Halfway along, they pass Wolff's armored car parked in the
garage block. Max points to the Picardie's upper floors and then to
the vehicle. The need for silence and caution could not be made any
plainer.

The service door opens into a windowless hallway. Empty crates
and boxes are stacked against one wall. Another door leads from
the hallway into the kitchen. The hallway is where deliveries of food
and other supplies are received. It is as far as it is possible to be from
the public and guest areas of the hotel. It is where Max can handle
the next step in safety. No one will see; no one will hear.

When all of them are inside, he locks the outer door and switches
on the overhead light. He sees faces pallid and taut with anxiety.
The men are young, almost as young as Sophie Carrière.

The briefing notes he collected from Laure Rioche on his visit
to the switchboard room yesterday tell him that they are British
bomber crew, all from one aircraft. But again his information is
limited: he does not know where their aircraft was brought down,
under what circumstances, whether they crash-landed or bailed

out. Their total combat crew could have been five or six strong, possibly more. The others might have been captured or perhaps they did not survive—something else he has no need or wish to know.

He turns to the tall man who seems to be their leader, the one who was the first to arrive at the archway.

"Do any of you speak French?"

He puts the question in English. The most common nationality that comes down the line is British. So far only four men have spoken French—two Canadians and two French pilots who had made their way to England when France fell and then joined British aircraft squadrons.

In terms of linguistic skills, these three young men prove to be as disappointing as the rest.

The airman shakes his head. "Sorry, no French."

Max continues in English. "You are not in uniform, so the Germans will say you are spies if they capture you. Spies are not sent to prisoner-of-war camps. They are simply shot—interrogated first, then shot."

"We know."

"While you are here you will do what I say—because I will shoot you if I have to. You understand?"

The airman has a resigned look, as if he has heard all this before. "We understand. Basically, everybody gets to shoot us."

Max gestures for them to sit on the crates. He takes the only chair and unfolds Laure's notes. The Browning remains in his other hand by way of warning and reminder.

"I will ask questions. You will not help each other."

There is no need for him to explain this deadly game that could end in the summary execution of any or all of the men. They will have been through some version of it before. They will already know that would-be escapers and evaders like them have been executed for failing to convince their hosts that they are genuine. They will have been told about the German tactic of planting agents to pose as Allied airmen when an aircraft is brought down. For Max it is significant that these three are all apparently from the same air-crew—meaning either that all of them are genuine or that all are infiltrators, German agents.

He begins with the leader.

"What is the name of your commanding officer?"

The questions are always different, unique to each individual or group admitted to the line. Sometimes they are trivial and everyday, sometimes technical. It depends on what is transmitted to Laure by London. Max trusts that they are based on information that no German imposter could know.

"He's called Harrison, Ted Harrison," replies the tall airman. "His name is really Edward but he calls himself Ted."

"He has a dog. Tell me what type and its name."

"Labrador. She's called Peggy."

Max turns to one of the others.

"What was your target destination on your last flight?"

The answer comes in a stammer. "M–Münster."

"What happened to your aircraft when it was about to be air-tested that day?"

The man is nervous. He glances at his leader, who turns away immediately, to avoid any suggestion of collusion.

"Faulty landing g–gear," the young man manages. In his nervous-ness he continues talking. "Unluck–unlucky omen. And it—"

Max raises a hand to silence him.

Now the final man.

"Tell me the name of the last person whose birthday you cele-brated on your base."

A moment's thought; then: "Jock MacIntyre." A grin directed at his companions. "We had a good night, that night."

"What is his work, his job?"

"Ground crew chief."

The questions continue until the check is complete. As far as Max can tell, the men are who and what they claim to be. He folds Laure's notes and puts them away.

"You will wait now," he instructs the three men.

He goes through to the kitchen, turning the key in the door behind him so that the men remain locked in the hallway.

What will happen now is not for them to see.

*   *   *

Max gives Duc Henri his due: the ill-starred aristocrat did nothing by halves. For his portrait he no doubt presented himself in his favorite attire, ensuring that posterity would remember him at his very best. He was not to know that posterity would come somewhat sooner than he anticipated. And when the masterpiece was complete, he did not stint on the magnificent frame surrounding it, an extravagant creation of gilded wood and gesso, fussy with laurel leaves and complex foliage and curlicues.

But not all the foliage is wood or plaster. Two of the large leaves on the right-hand side are made of solid iron, painted gold to match the rest of the frame.

Max pulls hard on both leaves together, drawing them towards himself. They rise smoothly from their bed of foliage. A solid clunk sounds, as of a spring-loaded mechanism releasing, and the portrait and its section of oak paneling swing clear from the wall, the right-hand side now open by several centimeters.

He opens the door fully. Within is a small area of landing, wide and deep enough for one person to stand on but no more.

He checks that the light switch and bulb are working. A steeply pitched flight of steps constructed of concrete and stone is revealed, falling abruptly away from the narrow landing to a depth of ten meters or more. The effect of such depth combined with the extreme angle of pitch is dizzying.

A single steel rail serves as banister. It does little to offset the hair-raising perspective of that deadly drop.

The strange aftermath of Henri's death—those rolling eyes and the speechless mouth—may well be nothing but legend. So also may be the claims of Henri's cruelty to his poor friar confessor.

But Henri's dungeon is another matter. Henri's dungeon is no legend. It is real enough.

Max returns to the rear hallway. He hands a strip of cloth to the tall airman and gestures with the pistol. Again, there is no need for explanation: the men have been through similar procedures before on their journey along the escape line. The airman ties the cloth in place as a blindfold. Max guides him at gunpoint through the kitchen and to the lobby. He helps him step over the high ledge beneath the portrait and places him safely inside Henri's doorway.

Only now does he remove the blindfold and switch on the light, so that the man can see where he is.

Their reactions are always the same, the reactions of the people that Max guides here, regardless of whether they are civilians or military personnel—reactions that are the natural and instinctive response to where they find themselves. Without warning they discover they are in a place where one false step—or a nudge from Max—will pitch them head first to a certain broken neck.

The British airman is no exception, for all his familiarity with vertiginous heights. Instinctively he tries to step back, but is stopped by the muzzle of the Browning in his back. He seizes hold of the steel banister and clings to it as the pistol urges him downward.

Max follows him down the steps, staying safely behind and above him, and gestures for him to open the heavy oak door at the bottom and enter the dungeon. When the man has found the light inside and switched it on, Max descends fully and locks him in.

The whole procedure has been done without a word being spoken.

He repeats the procedure with the other two airmen.

In the dungeon the men will find food and drinking water waiting for them, a barrel of water with which to wash, mattresses and bedding, and metal pails to serve as latrines—primitive arrangements but adequate.

When all the men have been delivered to the dungeon, Max swings Henri's portrait and the section of oak paneling back into place for the final time. The iron leaves recede neatly into the gilt foliage and the mechanism locks smoothly with its usual solid clunk, testimony to the fine workmanship of Henri's long-forgotten builder.

Max makes a last check of the lobby and the windowless hallway. There is no trace that anyone has been present in the hallway or that Henri's portrait has been disturbed.

And certainly Henri will tell no tales.

Once again knowledge has been restricted. The airmen may be captured at any stage of their onward journey from here. Among the information they will yield under interrogation—and they will yield such information—will be mention of a basement deep underground where they were hidden. But they will not be able to say where it was.

They will be ignorant of anywhere called Dinon-sur-Authie, because the guides who brought them here will have been careful never to have uttered the name or allowed them to see road signs, whether in French or German lettering. They can report only that they were taken to a large house in which Germans were staying. They will not be able to name the Hôtel Picardie, and there are many large houses in which Germans are resident.

Max also knows they will not be able to name him. They will be made to describe him, but tonight they are desperate and fearful, and in the hands of interrogators they will be in an even worse state. Any descriptions they provide, even without trying deliberately to mislead their interrogators, will be confused and unreliable. They will not even agree on whether Max wore a cap.

And none of them will tell of the portrait of Duc Henri, because none of them has seen it.

Nor have Pierre, Juliette or Auguste ever seen what is hidden behind that portrait. They have no reason to suspect that anything is hidden there. They do not know where or how Max hides his charges. Nor does Laure Rioche.

Need to know only. The golden rule.

With the airmen safely hidden, Max puts the Browning away and steps outside to clear his head. He returns to the archway, removes the cap and wipes his brow.

"What the hell are you up to?" whispers a voice from the darkness.

CHAPTER 28

HIS FIRST INSTINCT is to go for the Browning, but even as his hand moves towards it he is registering who has spoken.

He leaves the weapon where it is and turns to face her. He can make out only a dark silhouette.

"How did you get out?" he demands.

She meets the question with one of her own. "What kind of late-night guests were those I saw? They have a peculiar way of arriving."

He tries to assess risk and potential damage. So she has seen the airmen arrive, but she does not know who or what they are, nor how they got here—even if she saw the signal lights. She is outside now and hopefully that is where she was while he was questioning the men and taking them to the dungeon. All the blackout blinds are in place, they were in place throughout, and there are no windows in the rear service hallway, so she could not have seen anything that happened indoors, including what he did with Duc Henri's portrait. His questioning of the airmen was conducted in hushed tones, so she could not have overheard anything. She may not even speak English.

On the other hand, if her original objective was to flee the Picardie and Dinon, the fact that she is still here and has waited for him to reappear—with no guarantee that he would do so—is a measure of her determination to pry into matters that are none of her business.

He takes her back to his quarters and the bedroom. To his surprise she makes no protest. He switches on the dim light. When he sees the empty window frame, the scraped-out putty and the broken knife, it is all too obvious how she freed herself. He looks at the pane of glass with its sharp edges and corners, sees the state of her hands, a mass of open cuts and bruises, and shakes his head at the risk she has taken.

"You could have sliced through an artery."

"Then your problems would have been solved. No more Sophie Carrière causing trouble or dumping herself on you."

She leans back against the wall. She is quiet, deep in thought, head down, her face concealed by the curtain of hair. He waits, sensing that she has more to say. He is learning her ways.

She pushes the hair aside and looks at him.

"Let me save you the trouble of lying, Max. I know what you're doing, why you have people arriving in the middle of the night and why you've taken them into the hotel. Three men, all of them young, and they looked to me like military types. I know you're armed and I saw you search them. They didn't object to that, they let you do that as if it was what they expected, as meek as lambs. You took them in at gunpoint, just like you did with me. Again they didn't argue, even though they outnumbered you, because they expected that as well. This is your show and they know it. I think they're Allied servicemen. They're on the run and you're hiding them here, protecting them."

She stops, to see what he has to say. He says nothing.

"But you're doing more than just hiding them, aren't you? They're here because they need to get out of France, out of German-held territory, and back to wherever they belong, which is England I suppose. You can help them do that because you're running an escape network. That's what this place is—an escape line."

And there it is. He looks at her. That disturbing gaze is still fixed on him. She is many things but stupid is not one of them. Of course, he can deny everything. He can insist she has it all wrong. He can try inventing some story or other to account for what she has seen. And she will believe none of it.

"The last time I heard your opinion, I was a collaborator."

"So now you're not. Make the most of my good opinion while it lasts. Tell me the truth. I'm not even asking where you've hidden them—I just want to know if I'm right."

He knows they have reached a point of no return. If she tries to escape again and is captured, she will end up telling the Germans what she believes anyway—she will have no choice; they will force it from her, just as he warned. So much for his damage assessment.

But at least she does not know about Henri's dungeon, as she herself has made clear. Nor anything about the rest of the escape line before or beyond Dinon and the Picardie. All he can do now is dissuade her from further foolishness—the very behavior that might land her in Egon Wolff's hands. And the only way he can do that is if she knows how much is at stake.

So in the end he has no choice.

"You want the truth," he says. "Yes, the Picardie is part of an escape line. We move military personnel and civilians, we take them in and keep them safe until we can move them on. A couple of days here, a few nights, then they're gone, moved on to the next cell as soon as possible."

Her eyes are bright with triumph. "Military personnel? So I'm right. Allied fighters."

"In the early days it was soldiers who hadn't managed to escape from Dunkirk. Now it's mostly airmen who've been shot down or crash-landed."

"And the civilians—who are they? Jews?"

"Sometimes. They might be people who've spoken out against the Germans or are on a wanted list—intellectuals, academics, writers, politicians and officials who've refused to do the Germans' bidding—endangered individuals who need to get out of France or another occupied country—Belgium, the Netherlands. They might be one step ahead of arrest or they might have been arrested and managed to get away. And yes, from time to time there are Jews. Whoever they are, Jews or otherwise, if London clears them they join the line. In the same way as with military personnel, we receive them here and move them on as soon as it's safe to do so—safe for us, safe for them, and safe for the next part of the line, the next cell."

"You keep saying 'we'. You and who else?"

He shakes his head, denying her that information. He has told her enough—and that much only because of what she has worked out for herself. Now it is his turn to gather information.

"You told me your family was arrested at the beginning of the occupation. Arrested but then released. Are they still at liberty?"

She pauses for a long moment before replying. But reply she does, as if acknowledging that some kind of trade in truth has been agreed between them.

Her gaze is distant, unfocused.

"Roundups of Jews are nothing new in Paris. The first to be taken were foreign Jews. But recently the Germans have been turning their attention to French Jews like my family. Our mistake was not leaving the city at the very beginning, as soon as we knew the Germans were coming. We should have fled and not returned, like others who left and never came back. But not only fled Paris—we should have got out of France. A couple of months ago my mother and father were arrested again. They had to present themselves at their local gendarmerie—that's how the Germans get our French police to do their dirty work for them. It was the same police station that Papa, Maman and I had been taken to before."

"What about you? You weren't arrested this time?"

"I wasn't at home. I don't know if I'd been sent for as well. I missed curfew the previous night and had to stay with friends. When I got home that morning our neighbors told me what had happened. I tried to find out where my parents had been taken after the gendarmerie, but I got nowhere. I'm realistic now, I don't think I'll ever see them again. They're gone. I went into hiding. My friends and I had been talking for months about becoming involved with the Resistance. It took me a while to make contact with the right people, but that morning was when I made my decision."

The right people. He lets that pass without comment. No point riling her. Better to keep her talking. Certainly better than her usual bickering and complaints.

"You haven't mentioned your brother."

Another pause—a brief one this time, all the more decisive for its brevity.

"He died long before that."

Just as when she first spoke of the arrest of her family, her clipped reply makes it clear that she has said all she intends. His hope to keep her talking founders. He will get no more from her. Their trade in truth is at an end.

But he has heard enough anyway. Her family is gone—in all likelihood she is right to assume that her parents are dead. Her motives for joining the Resistance are clear. And equally clear is the callousness of the hard men in choosing her for their mission—not only untrained and untested, but also, it now turns out, only a matter of weeks after joining them.

She inhales and expels a deep breath, as if chasing from her mind the past and the memories she has summoned.

"This escape line," she says. "Right under the noses of your German guests. The last place they'd suspect anything of the sort."

"Which is why those German guests are so important to us. Do you understand now? Having them here is about more than extra food rations." He pauses, marking a change of direction. "Now I must ask something very important of you, Sophie."

But as with the existence of the escape line, she has worked that out for herself as well.

"Paris," she says.

"Yes, Paris. Under no circumstances should you tell them about any of this. Your Resistance cell might not be secure. I have my suspicions."

She looks as if she is about to argue, but he carries on.

"Whether you accept that or not, you must say nothing about what you've learnt tonight."

"I know that."

"Anything you tell Paris could jeopardize the lives of many people—"

"Max, I know."

"Good. And I must be sure you won't cause any trouble here, you won't do anything that could lead to your capture. Because you'll be interrogated and—"

"Max, please, I understand. Really, I do."

"No trouble here in the Picardie and not a word to Paris. I ask that of you."

There is amusement in her eyes, as though she would make one of her little games from his anxiety.

"All right, Max. I've got the point. No trouble, not a word to Paris. My lips are sealed. Look—you see?"

She raises a finger to her lips. Full lips, dark and glistening in the faint light of that weak bulb.

Like a fool he does what she says—he looks at her as the finger touches her lips. That is his mistake. Something in the room changes. Or perhaps it is something within himself, a misstep in the beat of his heart, a missed pulse. Suddenly there seems to be too little air in the small bedroom despite the missing window glass. He finds he is standing too close to her.

Or is it she who has moved?

He does not know how it happens, even afterwards he cannot unravel how it comes about, but in that moment she is in his arms, her slim body trembling against his.

Did he clasp her or did she come to him?

Her eyes have closed. The moment seems suspended in time and space, as though there is nothing in the world but this small room and the two of them. He hardly dares breathe but feels her breath on his cheek, feels the movement of her breasts as her chest rises and falls. Her lips touch his, brushing them so gently he might only be imagining it. He feels the warmth of her body and smells the fragrance that was here when he first came to her in this bedroom. A tense current of desire, of sensations and needs long forgotten, courses through his body.

How a man's life can tilt on its axis. How it can tumble beyond his control.

A warning rises to the surface of his mind. He tries to dismiss it but it is insistent. It is the conviction that this is wrong, that he must not allow it to happen. However the moment came about, whichever of them provoked it, he must end it.

He frees her from his embrace as gently as he can.

She is startled. She opens her eyes and he sees that he was right about their elusive colors: there are golds and greens within their gray ocean—an ocean in which he cannot tell whether he is swimming or sinking.

"What is it, Max?" Her voice is barely audible. "Is it because of her?"

A chill touches him. What is this? What does she know?

"Max, I found the photographs. I don't know who she is, but—"

He steps back, taking her injured hands in his.

"Stay here now, Sophie. Don't try to leave again on your own. I'll come back."

She does not hide her distress. Does not or cannot.

"If you leave now, Max, you won't come back to me. I know you won't."

"I will. I promise."

"You promise? Do you keep your promises, Max?"

"Always."

As he leaves the room he knows Geneviève is there, watching and listening.

"Always," he whispers.

*　*　*

There is still an hour or so until dawn. He fetches a blanket and tries to doze on a sofa in the lobby. But his efforts are useless; no sleep comes to him.

Eventually he gives up and goes to the washroom behind the kitchen. He washes, shaves, dresses in fresh clothing and returns to the lobby. To wait for morning and the meeting with Egon Wolff.

CHAPTER 29

OUTSIDE HER PRISON a new day is beginning. Sunlight falls through the empty window. The mirror casts its reflection and the slow progress of the oval of light across the walls recommences.

The door is no longer locked—he has given up on that—but this bedroom is a prison more than ever now.

Once, she hated him for imprisoning her here. Now her imprisonment is worse; it is no longer defined and bounded by these four walls, for he has imprisoned her poor heart, he has put it in chains. It will bear the weight of those chains wherever she goes and whatever she does. There will be no digging her way free from them.

But she cannot hate him for that.

Her eyes close, shutting out the morning light and bringing a different morning in its place.

Why must she lose those she loves?

She dreams of the dead.

* * *

It is that June morning when the Germans marched into Paris. The morning when they took her city without a shot being fired.

The pavements on either side of the Champs-Élysées—its entire length, all the way from the Arc de Triomphe—are packed with

people. She can barely make her way through the crowds, so dense
are they. Most shops are boarded up, but some cafés are making the
most of the extra trade. German soldiers have been posted along
the route to maintain order. Perhaps also because violence is feared:
she notes with a shiver of fear the occasional machine-gun unit.

Yet alongside those Parisians who are weeping at the Germans'
arrival, she sees many clapping and cheering in the sunshine to
welcome them. She wants to claw their eyes out, those idiots who
are laughing and celebrating, she wants to tell them that today is
not a day of festivities, today is the day when the honor of France
has been lost.

The numbers of the invaders are as incalculable as grains of sand.
On and on they pour into her city, sweeping along the wide avenue,
which has been cleared of other traffic. Could any country on earth
stand against such numbers? There are more soldiers than she has
ever seen in her life—on foot, in vehicles, on horseback, proceeding
in perfect discipline. Military bands, their musicians mounted on
beautiful white horses—too beautiful for war. Lorries and trucks,
military vehicles of every kind—tanks with tracks instead of
wheels, inventions from hell that clank and roar with a racket that
makes the ground quake, and other huge armored machines,
clumsy and terrifying, with great gun barrels on top and large
enough to carry ranks of soldiers standing to attention on their
flanks. Uncountable numbers of gun carriages, endless cortèges of
motorcycles. The noise is such that she can barely think.

On and on the Germans come, marching, cantering, borne by
their rumbling machines of war, until her head throbs with the
relentless din and the heat and the stink in the stale summer air and
the tightly packed bodies around her.

And now she sees Gérard, catches sight of him weaving through
the press of people and coming in her direction. Although she
waves, he does not see her. She knows at once that something is

amiss. His head is down as he pushes through the crowd, his shoulders hunched, exactly the way he used to skulk when he was up to mischief as a child.

In the road near her stands a group of German officers, stiff and hot in their uniforms. One of them must be very important, for he carries a silver-handled cane that he raises in salute from time to time as the triumphal parade passes.

Suddenly there is a disturbance in the crowd where she glimpsed Gérard, a ripple of activity. She sees agitated faces, people turning, mouths open wide as if they are shouting. Are they frightened? Are they calling out a warning? She cannot hear them over the din, so she cannot tell. All she knows is that something is wrong.

Gérard is in the road. He has pushed his way through. He is running towards the group of officers, who have not seen him. German soldiers pound after him. They are shouting but again she cannot hear, their voices drowned by the noise of the parade.

But she can see. And she sees that they have guns.

At last one of the officers realizes what is happening. He yells—soundlessly, to her ears—draws his gun and rushes forward, towards Gérard, shielding the man with the silver-topped cane, pushing him back to safety.

The officer shoots. Gérard shoots. The German's face explodes in a fountain of blood.

Gérard lies crumpled on the road, in a spreading pool of blood. The German has fallen to his knees beside him.

The parade continues. On and on the Germans come.

Paris is theirs.

Gérard is dead.

CHAPTER 30

"THEY'RE HERE," MAX tells Bruno. "They came last night."

It is not long after dawn. Bruno has just arrived at the Picardie and the two of them are in the barn, safe from German eyes and ears. In any case, Wolff and his aide are still asleep; Max has been upstairs to check on them.

Bruno lights his cigarette.

"That's good," he says. "How many?"

"Three, exactly as we were told. British airmen. They're uninjured and appear to be in good health. They were unarmed and I've carried out the usual identity checks. They shouldn't present any complications."

"Good. We've got enough of those already."

"More than you think. Sophie got herself free. She was out here when they were delivered. She saw them."

A plume of cigarette smoke greets this. "Damnation!"

"And she figured out it's an escape line."

Bruno rolls his eyes and swears again. "I warned you she'd be trouble."

"She doesn't know where the men are. She doesn't know about the dungeon."

"Thank God for that at least."

"There's no telling how she'll be today. She might be calm or she might be even more on edge than her usual state."

Bruno gives him a long look. "More on edge because of what she's seen? Why? She knows we're not collaborators now, so why should she be more on edge?" He stares suspiciously at Max. "Or is it something else? Has something happened with her?"

"Look in on the airmen when you can. I appreciate it could be difficult if Virginie and Paul—"

But Bruno will not let go. "I know how to do this, Max. You don't need to spell it out. Tell me—what's happened with you and her?"

"Nothing happened. I have a meeting with Wolff this morning. I told you something's going on with him and High Command. I think I might be about to find out what it is."

"Like I said, we should be worried."

"We'll see, Bruno, we'll see."

*   *   *

At breakfast Wolff behaves as on any other morning. He is polite, thanks Max when his food arrives, converses quietly with his aide while they eat.

As he is leaving the dining room, he stops beside Max.

"I propose an hour from now for our meeting, Monsieur. I hope that is convenient for you."

He does not bother waiting for Max's reply. He settles his cap in place and strides off.

*   *   *

The morning is fine and bright, as innocent as any summer morning could be, the sky a delicate blue glaze from horizon to horizon. The day will be hot again; when Max goes to the barn and fetches his bicycle the sun's rays are already warm on his back. The blackbird greets him with its full-throated song as he mounts the bicycle. He pauses for a moment to listen, then cycles from the barn, out through the gateway, and makes for Dinon and, along the way, Wolff's roadblocks.

He watches for Geneviève ahead of him on rue de la République, but she is not there.

PART TWO

REPRISAL

CHAPTER 31

"Monsieur le Maire. You will be seated."

Wolff's face gives nothing away. He joins Max at the conference table in his office, bringing with him a thin cardboard folder. In a corner of the room a stenographer taps at the keys of his machine. So the meeting is to be minuted, something that has not been done since the first meetings between Wolff and Max.

Two armed troopers stand by the door. Again, it is the first time this has happened since those early days.

There is no small talk. Wolff comes straight to the point. The stenographer taps busily, a muted pitter-patter of keys.

"Monsieur Duval, I have received orders from Military High Command which I am instructed to share with you in your capacity as mayor of Dinon-sur-Authie. They have been issued by General von Stülpnagel, Military Commander of France. I can add that they comply with the express wishes of the Führer himself."

"Dinon is flattered to have your Führer's attention."

Wolff removes two typed sheets of paper from the folder and scans the top one, even though he must already be versed in its content.

"First, a system of nominating notables among the civilian population will be applied with immediate effect to the town and commune of Dinon-sur-Authie. These notables are to be defined as—"

"I know what notables are."

Wolff disregards the interruption. He is working to a script. Everything he says will be in those minutes, to be pored over and checked by avenue Kléber.

"These notables are influential individuals who occupy a prominent position within the community or who have significant commercial, religious, or civic stature. The Reich reserves to itself the right without dispute to nominate these notables. They will be guarantors against civil unrest or malicious behavior directed at military or civilian representatives of the Reich, at its property or at establishments, production facilities, transport systems and utilities that assist or support the Reich or are engaged in activities of any kind on the Reich's behalf."

"Guarantors, Major? Call them what they'll really be—hostages. You've never imposed this system of control."

"True. Dinon has enjoyed a privileged position. But a privilege is not an entitlement, and this particular privilege is now withdrawn."

Wolff has picked up the second typed sheet. He does not look at Max but keeps his gaze on the closely typed page.

"The second part of my orders is this. Following the recent assassination of two loyal and courageous soldiers of the Reich, and Dinon's failure to render adequate assistance in apprehending the escaped assassin, positive action will now be put in hand. If by midnight tomorrow, the assassin has not surrendered himself or been handed over—preferably alive but dead will do—then ten citizens of Dinon will be executed by firing squad."

Max rises to his feet.

"Major, that would go against every international law, against all the laws of warfare, not to mention basic human morality. Not even you can do this, not even the damned German Reich."

He is aware of the troopers behind him stepping forward. He hears the slap of hands on rifles.

Wolff looks up calmly from the sheet of paper. "You will remain seated, Monsieur. The notes of this meeting will not record how you referred to the Reich just now. This is the only time I will exercise such discretion, so I advise you to show respect in your choice of language."

The muzzle of a rifle presses into Max's back, another into his neck. He sits down.

"Major, I've told you my citizens have nothing to do with the killing of your men. They don't know who the assassin is, except that he's not one of them. They don't know where he is. He could even be dead—you said one of your troopers returned fire. My people can't hand him over; they simply can't do what you want."

"You are wrong, Monsieur. I know you are wrong."

There is something odd in his insistence. But Max has no opportunity to consider it or make sense of it, because the Feldkommandant has returned to the typed sheet.

"Those to be executed will comprise four of Dinon's notables, nominated by me on behalf of the Reich, and six ordinary citizens chosen at random. The latter are to be taken into custody immediately. These six will be executed at midnight tomorrow. As a concession, the notables will not be taken into custody immediately but are trusted to present themselves of their own accord at midnight tomorrow. They will be executed twenty-four hours later."

There is no concession here, despite what Wolff pretends. The four notables are to remain free only so that they can exert their personal influence to secure the handing over of the missing assassin. Wolff knows that they will not try to flee or go into hiding because others will simply be put to death in their place.

Their executions will be delayed for twenty-four hours so that they can be interrogated to see if they yield information on the missing assassin or any other useful intelligence. The six other citizens will also be interrogated, in the period between their arrest and their execution.

Wolff sets the sheet of paper aside. But he has a final pronouncement to deliver.

"Monsieur, I hope these executions can be avoided. I am sure you feel the same. But if they cannot, High Command has ordered that they should be followed by more executions at intervals which I will have authority to decide, and that this further action should continue until the assassin is in custody."

The nightmare is complete. There will be as many deaths as Wolff wishes or until he gets what he wants—actually, until avenue Kléber gets what it wants. Max searches for humanity in the Feldkommandant's face, a hint that there is some way out of this, but the scarred face could be carved from marble. Wolff will say only what Military High Command has authorized him to say. The evidence will be in those minutes, every word he utters. He will be held to account. Any error on his part, any shortcoming, any deviation from avenue Kléber's orders, will be recorded there forever.

"Major, if you allow these executions to go ahead, the Resistance, the very organization you fear, will take root here in Dinon and neither you nor your men will ever rest easy again."

"I will take that risk. I do not fear the Resistance."

"You should. The Reich will be under threat minute by minute. You'll fear every citizen of Dinon—men, women, even children— as potential killers. Every time you or your men turn your backs you'll be waiting for a bullet. Day and night. There'll be acts of sabotage—power supply, vehicles, garrison barracks, rail lines, communications equipment, perhaps even your armory. Dinon will become a place in which every side street and alley, every hedge and barn might conceal a résistant with a bomb or a submachine gun. Every visit by your men to a café or bar, even to your own cinema and brothel, will be a venture to be feared by them, not enjoyed. Your men will never know peace of mind again, neither on duty nor in their leisure time. Is this what you want?"

Wolff is unyielding. "I do not accept any of what you say. It will not happen because I do not believe that your citizens know nothing. I know for a fact that the assassin is still in Dinon—whether he belongs to Dinon or was sent here—and someone is hiding him, protecting him. Let them hand him over and there will be no executions—nor any of these consequences you are predicting. I am confident there is someone in Dinon who is prepared to do the right thing in this crisis and deliver the assassin to the justice he deserves—whether that assassin is neighbor or outsider. On the day you and I first met, the day I came to Dinon, you asked for my assurance that your citizens would be safe, and I gave you my word. We have not always agreed on the finer details of Dinon's day-to-day governance, but I believe you will agree that I have kept my word. Now it is your turn to find a way to make your citizens safe, Monsieur Duval."

"But, Major—"

It is useless. Wolff's patience is at an end. He raises a hand to silence Max.

"Monsieur Duval, we can accomplish nothing more here. The rest is up to the people of Dinon and you as their mayor. This meeting is concluded. Any future meetings that prove necessary will be formal and minuted, as this one has been. You will of course receive a copy of the notes of today's meeting."

"As you wish, Major."

"Further, I will publish a decree so that your citizens are clear on the nature of the steps being taken and how the executions can be avoided if they act promptly to bring the assassin to justice. You and I will see then which of us is right. In the meantime, you will need this."

Wolff passes the cardboard folder across the table. The stenographer's soft tap-tapping has ceased. There is now a thick silence in the room, heavy and oppressive, as if death is already present.

Max flips the folder open. It contains a third and final sheet of paper. At the top is the black Reich letterhead of eagle and swastika. Underneath are the names of the nine men and one woman who will be executed.

Max closes the folder and passes it back to Wolff. He has no need to keep the sheet of paper; he will remember those ten names, the names of the four notables and the six other citizens. How could he not? He knows every one of the so-called ordinary citizens and their families. He knows their histories, for they are part of Dinon's history and his own. Wolff may call them ordinary, but they are not ordinary to those who love them.

Among them is Paul Burnand, the Picardie's kitchen lad. He is the youngest of those to be arrested and executed. His first romance will not blossom after all; obnoxious little Jacques Dompnier will have nothing to worry about.

As for the notables, Max's own name heads that list. The others are Auguste Froment, Pierre Hamelin and Juliette Labarthe.

CHAPTER 32

As Max is leaving the Kommandantur, he hears the roar of trucks moving at speed through nearby streets. The arrests of the six citizens listed for execution tomorrow midnight are already in hand. Even though the fate awaiting them is not yet known to them or their families, there will be widespread terror. But there is nothing he can do about that. What possible reassurance can he offer? He feels useless.

He cycles from street to street, trying to follow the sound of the vehicles. In rue des Chênes a truck cuts in front of him and skids to a halt. The tailgate crashes open, there are shouts of "Schnell! Schnell!" as a gang of armed troopers vault to the ground, boots ringing on the cobblestones. They disappear into an alley that leads to a cluster of cottages around a small courtyard.

One of the men on Wolff's death list lives there. Max cycles on in an attempt to follow the squad but is stopped by troopers who have remained in the street to stand guard. He argues, insisting that as mayor he must be allowed to speak to his citizen. He doubts it will get him anywhere, but perhaps he can stay arguing long enough to snatch a word with the man as he is brought out.

Even that strategy fails. One of the troopers advances on him and pushes him away at gunpoint.

*　*　*

He will go to Auguste and Pierre and Juliette, to tell them what is to happen, but first he needs time and solitude in which to weigh life and death. He cycles away from the center of town, away from the little houses of brick and the cottages of stone, out past the fire station, the Germans' brothel and their cinema.

He has known these streets and lanes and shaded alleys all his life, but he sees them this morning with a painful clarity, as though his eyes have been only half open until now. He will shortly depart forever from these familiar places when Egon Wolff and German High Command have their way. The life of these streets will continue without him. The reality of that is hard.

But this death sentence is not his alone. Nor even only of Auguste, Pierre and Juliette and the others on Wolff's list. The Feldkommandant has been given the authority to keep going, to continue with the executions until he gets what High Command wants: namely, Sophie Carrière. And he will use that power.

But there is one person who can stop him, who can prevent all the deaths by delivering Sophie Carrière to him. That person is Max Duval.

Why should he not do that? He would only be doing what he has sworn he would always do: protect the people of his little town. It is what his citizens expect of him, and it is no more than they deserve. He can lift Dinon's death sentence.

There is a further consideration, one that he warned Sophie to expect, and it applies just as much to himself as to her. It is what he and the others in the Dinon cell live with every day of their lives— the knowledge that everyone, sooner or later, breaks under interrogation. Everyone. No exceptions. So even if he does not give Sophie up willingly, he will end up betraying her anyway.

And he might give Wolff more than Sophie. She is the only prize of which the German is aware, but what if Max also betrays the escape line, admits to its existence and the work of the Dinon cell? Since the cell is a cut-out, the line itself would be protected, but revealing its existence would stall its work for months, possibly impairing it forever even if its operators remain safe.

Certainly the lives of the three British airmen would be forfeit unless they can be moved on immediately.

And then there are Laure Rioche and Bruno. Would he betray them as well?

Yet with one act he can prevent this chain of death. All he has to do is give Wolff what he wants—not the escape line, not the airmen, not Bruno and Laure, but the one thing the German knows about, the only prize he has fixed upon. And do it now, while there is still time.

All it takes is for Max to make the decision. All it takes is the sacrifice of that one life, to save so many other lives.

After all, these death sentences have come about not because of the escape line, not because of errors or carelessness on the part of the Dinon cell or any other section of the line, not even because of successful infiltration by German agents. These deaths will be the fault of those who had no business sending their violence to Dinon in the first place—the hard men in Paris who manipulated Jean-Luc and Sophie Carrière.

A single life. That is all it would take to prevent so many deaths. The life of Sophie Carrière.

An image rises before him, unbidden: Sophie in the condition in which he saw Jean-Luc in Wolff's posters, her face white, the cascade of hair matted with blood, her eyes fogged and dead, the defiance of her gaze gone forever.

Then comes a voice, clear and unmistakable.

"Would you do that, Max? Would you sacrifice that life? Could you do that?"

But when he turns to the sound, Geneviève is nowhere to be seen.

CHAPTER 33

HE FINDS AUGUSTE bent over his long table in the print room, examining bits of ink-darkened metal through a large magnifying glass. Hundreds of pieces of metal type cover the entire tabletop, awaiting his attention.

"Trying to work out what I can still use or repair," Auguste explains as he clicks a piece of type into its wooden tray and straightens up.

"No more posters for a while, then," says Max. "Not even for Wolff's latest decree."

Auguste sets the magnifying glass down and looks properly at him. "What decree is that?"

"You may want to sit down."

"Your news is that bad? I'll stand. Get on with it."

Auguste listens without interruption. When Max finishes, the printer manages an unhappy smile.

"So I have the honor of being declared a notable." His voice falters.

"A dubious honor, Auguste."

"Perhaps it'll make my Marie proud. She's never been proud of me. Did you know that? She thinks what I do is trivial. My official work, I mean. She doesn't know about the unofficial side of things.

Has always thought *La Voix de Dinon* is a bit of a joke. Even more of a joke, a sick joke, since Wolff took it over. Maybe now I can be a hero for her. That's good, Max, you know."

"Auguste—"

"I suppose Wolff expects us to yield in terror to his threats, the way he terrified me yesterday. He thinks fear of a German bullet will make us hand over the only surviving patriot in Dinon who has lifted a finger in defense of France—I know you don't agree with that view of the gunman, I haven't forgotten our little chat. And I've never believed he was gone from Dinon. I didn't fall for what you said, that Wolff wouldn't track him down."

"Why not?"

"I reckoned Wolff wouldn't stop, that he'd come up with some kind of vile tactic. And he has—though I never foresaw anything as contemptible as this."

"I don't think it's his idea. Military High Command is behind it."

"Same difference. Anyway, since our chat, I've been giving some thought to what a coward I've been. And I'm ashamed. So this is my chance for my cowardice to end. I must disappoint our Feldkommandant—I'll be proud to give my life for the patriot he's hunting. I'd feel the same even if I was in a position to hand him over. I'd be proud to protect him. I honor that résistant. If only we had more like him. If only I was brave enough myself. What have I done for France? Forged a few identity cards for men and women who might or might not make it to safety and who then might or might not continue fighting or bombing the Germans."

"What you've done is hardly the work of a coward, Auguste."

"When I tried to go a little further, all I managed to do was provide a couple of bicycles—and then I caught it in the neck from you for making even that small contribution."

"You know what was at stake."

"I don't deny it. But maybe this is my opportunity to do better. That's how I feel about Wolff and his ultimatum. My regret isn't that I must die for France; it's only that I won't see a communist France first. I've never been allowed to tell Marie about our work—my work—with the escape line. But if I can summon the courage to walk out in front of a firing squad, maybe that's enough to make her just a little proud of me. What do you think?"

Max sighs. Each of the condemned ten, both ordinary citizens and notables alike—himself included—must find their own individual way to be at peace with what is to come. Auguste's way is as valid as any.

"Everyone in Dinon will be proud of you, Auguste. Not only Marie. But first there is another matter. We have some unfinished business. I need you to perform one last task for the escape line. You said you could still do that, you said you still have what you need."

The little printer blinks up at him as his meaning sinks in. "Are you telling me our three guests have come after all? Are you saying my usual services are still required?"

"Urgently. This evening."

Auguste beams. "Dear Max. One last opportunity to spit in Wolff's eye—even in Herr Hitler's eye. What better way to go?"

He clicks another piece of type into place.

*　*　*

Juliette Labarthe gazes through the pharmacy window at the sunny street outside, where her granddaughter is playing with friends. Close by, three troopers, rifles slung over their shoulders, are stopping people as they pass by, questioning them and examining identity papers. The children play on, heedless of the adult world.

Max finishes the account of his meeting with Wolff.

"That explains this morning's arrests," Juliette says. She steps back from the window. "What about the escape line, what happens to it? Presumably it has to be suspended until we're . . . replaced."

"It will be."

He decides to say nothing about interrogation and the possible exposure of the line and the cell—as likely by Juliette herself as by anyone.

"But our part in the line can't be suspended just yet," he adds. "We had arrivals last night."

"Well, that's good—but of all the impossible timing. So what do we do?"

"You should alert your contacts—we need them to be ready for an urgent handover."

"How urgent?"

"Tomorrow night."

She sucks in a sharp breath. "Short notice. But how can we do that? You said that's when we're supposed to present ourselves for arrest—"

"I know. But tomorrow night it has to be. And it won't be a normal handover."

He explains in detail what must happen and its exact timing.

"I'll do my part," she says. She returns to the window to watch the children.

"Look at them, Max. The little ones accept this as the natural order. We're raising a generation who might never know anything but a world where a person can be snatched away without warning, where armed strangers control our streets and our lives."

She removes her spectacles and rubs her eyes.

"Max, listen. I mustn't end up before a firing squad. I'm not strong enough for that—I'll beg for my life, and I don't want to do that. I don't want my daughter and grandchild to know I did that, I don't want them to have to live with that shame."

He was right not to frighten her with talk of interrogation.

"So you think we must find the assassin and surrender him?"

"No! I'm not talking about that." She puts on the spectacles and frowns up at him. "I'm talking about the nature of Wolff's threat—a firing squad. I'm saying that I have no intention of dying the way he wants me to."

She gazes at the glazed cabinets behind her, less well stocked since Wolff's raid, some of them damaged and chipped, but their shelves still carrying a good supply of bottles and jars.

"You're forgetting I'm a pharmacist, Max. There are ways to avoid such an end. Dignified, peaceful ways. Ways to go to rest with no more distress than falling into a gentle sleep. I could show you a score of alternatives, all within easy reach. Ways of cheating—"

She breaks off. Her hand flies to her mouth in a belated effort to take back her clumsy words. She is crimson with embarrassment.

"I'm sorry, Max, so sorry. That was thoughtless of me. What a fool I am. Please forgive me."

He shakes his head. "It's nothing. There's nothing to forgive."

"I wasn't thinking."

"It's in the past, Juliette. Let's you and I deal with the present. Are you telling me you wouldn't hand over the assassin? Assuming we could, that is."

She is subdued now, but her response is still firm.

"To hand him over would be the most shameful act of all."

*　*　*

Max watches as Pierre Hamelin runs a fingertip across the vials in the drawer of his medical bag, counting or checking them off mentally. He crosses the room, unlocks a cabinet similar to those in Juliette Labarthe's pharmacy, selects a vial, and adds it to the drawer.

"Do you think it significant that Wolff has chosen us as the first notables to be executed?" he asks. "All of us cell members?"

Max shakes his head. "I don't think so. He has avenue Kléber on his back. If he knew anything about the cell, if he suspected anything, he wouldn't wait until tomorrow midnight to have us in his custody. He'd arrest us right now. And he hasn't included Bruno. In fact, my hope is that Bruno will take over from me and rebuild the cell—if he survives."

Pierre frowns. "What do you mean, 'if he survives'?"

"If none of us names him."

"Ah, you expect us to be interrogated. And of course we will be. Well, if Bruno remains safe despite that, and if he's willing to carry on, I can arrange for someone to contact him when the dust has settled."

When the dust has settled. Max marvels at him. Pierre is speaking of his own death.

"You're very calm about this, Pierre."

The doctor chuckles softly. "Why shouldn't I be? At my age, death holds no terrors. Every morning is a surprise to me, a day I didn't expect to see." He snaps the bag shut. "So now I know how many mornings I have left. Few of us have that advantage. I consider myself fortunate."

Max puts his hand gently on his friend's arm. There seems to be no flesh or muscle there at all, only bone.

"Pierre, I want your view on something. You've dedicated yourself to saving lives. The man who committed this crime against the Reich, surely he's exactly what Wolff says—an assassin, a murderer, someone who takes lives. And puts innocent people in harm's way.

That's what has happened here. It's what we've tried with all our might to avoid in Dinon. In your heart don't you think he should be brought to justice?"

"I'm not sure I follow you, Max. Exactly what are you asking me?"

"If we could find him and hand him over, ten lives would be saved immediately, many more over time if Wolff continues to execute. What do you say to that, as a saver of lives? Surely so many lives outweigh one?"

The old man's gaze is acute. "Max, tread carefully. You call me a saver of lives. But I also kill, even if only at one remove. So do you. Each time we send an Allied airman to safety so that he can fight again or bomb another target in Germany—especially if it's a city and the victims are civilians—we become killers along with him. None of us is innocent. Not you, not me, none of us."

Max knows that he himself has followed this line of self-accusation.

"As for weighing multiple lives against one," continues Pierre, "by handing the assassin over we'd be caving in to Wolff's demands. In effect we'd be aiding Germany's occupation of our country."

"But how else can Wolff be stopped?"

"That I don't know, but there's a moral case to consider. It runs as follows. The Germans have no right to be here. Therefore, all their actions in support of their occupation are morally reprehensible. What's more, if we ourselves act in compliance with their immorality, our actions are equally wrong. The soil in which those actions grow is tainted, and so would they be."

"So we can't surrender the man Wolff's looking for?"

"Cannot and must not, according to that particular moral analysis."

"Then we must die. Not only these first ten but as many more as Wolff decides to execute."

"I don't know, Max—that judgment is too weighty for my old shoulders. But none of this matters."

"It doesn't?"

"No. Because it's purely hypothetical." Pierre hefts the medical bag and gives Max that penetrating look again. "Bearing in mind that we're not in a position to hand the killer over, are we?"

Max accompanies him outside. There are Germans wherever he looks.

"There must be another way, Pierre, a different view."

"Perhaps there is. Seek a second opinion by all means. But why assume it will offer more palatable guidance? And now you must excuse me—I have patients to see and limited time in which to see them, grateful though I am to have such warning."

Max pauses as he passes the surgery window. The little Chinese mannequin still stands calmly watching the troubled world outside. It appears to be smiling. Max moves on a few paces and looks again. Now the strange little thing is frowning at him.

Of one point he is convinced. There has to be a way to resolve the dilemma that Pierre has described, a way to give Wolff what he wants without being complicit in his crime. There must be another point of view. There always is. It all depends on where the observer is standing. A simple matter of perspective. Like the mannequin's ambiguous smile.

He must find that different perspective.

He mounts his bicycle and departs. He puts from his mind the memories of Geneviève that Juliette reawakened.

Or tries to.

CHAPTER 34

HE IS CONSCIOUS of many eyes following him as he makes his way back to place de la Mairie. Clearly the word is out: the reason for the arrests is known, and with it the fate that awaits him and the others.

Sure enough, a little crowd has gathered outside the Kommandantur and mairie. The sickening poster of Jean-Luc is still there, but that is not what has people's attention today. In the noticeboard is a typed letterheaded notice setting out High Command's orders. It is solidly Germanic in its thoroughness and degree of detail. Max reads through it. Everything is there—the introduction of the system of nominating notables, the reason for today's arrests, the reiterated demand for the assassin to be handed over, alive or dead, the identities of the six citizens and four notables scheduled for death, the timings of their executions, the threat of more executions to follow if necessary.

Wolff's confident signature adds the final flourish.

In his office, Max drafts a formal request for permission to visit the six men in custody. Hortense types it up and carries it the few paces across the shared entrance hall to the Kommandantur. Ten minutes later a reply arrives. Max's request has been refused.

"And we know why, don't we?" huffs Hortense.

Max nods. The interrogations have begun.

In a separate letter some minutes later, Wolff informs Max that with immediate effect he and his aide will no longer be resident in the Picardie. Arrangements will be made to fetch their belongings. Max is requested to prepare a final account. Final in more ways than one.

*   *   *

Max visits the families of the six who have been arrested and will be first to be executed. There is no comfort he can offer the families, and he knows that pretending otherwise would only exacerbate their agony. The most he can do is offer solidarity, hoping that some strength can come from shared grief.

But he has misjudged his Dinonnais. Comfort is not what the families are seeking; and they have all the solidarity they need—with each other and with the neighbors and family members who have already gathered in each home when he calls.

But there is a darker aspect to their mood, one that would please the hard men in Paris.

"We should join the armed struggle now," says the wife of one of the men in custody. "That's the only hope left to us. We've tried your way, Max, but you can see it hasn't worked. Not even for you. It's time for a different way."

Other families are equally firm: "Even if someone knows who this résistant is and turns him in, who can believe Wolff will keep his word?"

"I'll take up arms myself if I have to," says one young woman. "I've never shot a gun, but it can't be so hard if these wooden-headed Boche can do it."

But the most uncompromising of all is Louise Burnand, widowed mother of young Paul.

"I want Paul to be released, naturally I do," she tells Max. "But it can't be done. Even if Wolff gets the man he's after, he'll just come up with some other excuse to execute all of you. That's what he's really after. My Paul will die, just as you will, Max, just as the others will. It would be treachery for us to surrender the résistant. If I could die in Paul's place, I would. If I could die instead of you, Max, I would. But I can't die for either of you. You must both go to what awaits you, for you go in the very best of causes. Vive la France!"

The pattern of defiance and determination is repeated with every man and woman he speaks to that day in Dinon's streets and alleys and squares, in its cafés and bars, its little shops and warehouses, in the timber yard—wherever he goes.

These are the plain, unheroic people of Dinon, the heart and soul of France, people beaten down by hunger, worn to a thread by the occupier's demands; but not one of them says that the life of their neighbor or friend or fellow citizen is worth more than the life of the man who killed one of their oppressors. No one is willing to enter into the exchange that Wolff is demanding.

There is dismay, of course, at what is to happen. There is no shortage of tears, no lack of sympathy, for Max and the others. And there is fear, because no one knows who else will die or how many deaths there will be. How can Wolff be stopped? For that matter, *can* he be stopped?

By the time Max has finished his rounds it is clear that his town has made its decision. Wolff said that what happens next is up to him and the people of Dinon. Max has heard Dinon's view. So now it is up to him.

CHAPTER 35

WHEN HE RETURNS to the mairie, the minutes of the meeting with Wolff are on his desk. This copy is in French, since that was the language in which the meeting was held.

He is not particularly interested in the document. Experiencing the meeting was bad enough; why relive it on paper? He scans the document with a fraction of his attention and sets it aside.

But an uneasiness comes over him, a restless feeling that something here does not fit, that he has missed something. But what? He is not even sure that it has anything to do with the meeting or those neatly typed notes, but for want of any other clue or place to start he retrieves the document and begins to look through it again.

As he reads, he hears again the subdued pitter-patter of the stenographer's keys as Wolff's words and his own are plucked from the air and imprinted on pages that will be studied, in their German version, by faithful servants of Reich High Command.

And as he reads, a pattern slowly begins to emerge. Or is he deluding himself? He begins yet again, reading carefully, line by line. His pulse quickens. He rises from his desk, closes the door between his office and Hortense's, a rare signal that he is not to be disturbed.

The stenographer's work cannot be faulted. It is accurate. One by one, Max marks the passages that take his attention—passages that he soon becomes convinced are the cause of that uneasiness within him. All of them Wolff's words. And no man chooses his words with greater care than Egon Wolff.

Any one passage on its own would signify nothing. But all of them taken together, that is another matter—provided it is Max who brings them together. Max and only Max; only he can do that, he realizes, only he can read between those lines. Was that Wolff's intention? Significantly, none of the passages would ring alarm bells in avenue Kléber, none would mean anything to those faithful servants of the Reich as they comb through the record of the meeting.

The first passage records the moment when Max insisted that the people of Dinon knew nothing about the killer, an assertion he had made before, and frequently. This time, however, Wolff did not let the claim pass unchallenged. He was insistent:

"You are wrong, Monsieur. I know you are wrong."

It was as if he possessed—or believed he possessed—irrefutable evidence of some kind. But how could that be?

Then there was the question of the killer's whereabouts—and his origins:

"I know for a fact that the assassin is still in Dinon—whether he belongs to Dinon or was sent here..."

In those words, Wolff was allowing the possibility that the killer was not from Dinon—the first time he had done so. Not only that, but he even went so far as to allude to it a second time:

"... whether that assassin is neighbor or outsider..."

As for his conviction that the killer was still here in Dinon, how could he be so confident?

"I know for a fact..."

Was this more than mere stubbornness?

"I am confident there is someone in Dinon who is prepared to do the right thing in this crisis and deliver the assassin to the justice he deserves..."

Then came the Feldkommandant's final cryptic remark:

"Now it is your turn to find a way to make your citizens safe, Monsieur Duval."

And with that final part of the riddle, something clicks into place in Max's mind, like Auguste Froment's little pieces of metal type fitting into their tray.

CHAPTER 36

AN HOUR LATER Max is passing along a quiet residential lane on his way out to the Picardie when he becomes aware of the sound of raised voices.

He lets the bicycle coast to a stop. The source of the racket is a substantial detached villa set behind high walls and hedges. It is the home of police chief Jacques Dompnier. Windows are open wide on this sultry evening, allowing everything to be heard.

A family row is in full swing. Dompnier is shouting and swearing, there are crashes and bangs as a door or item of furniture feels the weight of his boot. Two female voices, wailing and sobbing, rise and fall between his shouts.

It is not hard to guess what the fracas is about: Yvette, Dompnier's daughter, is distraught over Paul Burnand's arrest and impending execution. Sure enough, Dompnier mentions the boy by name several times. And not flatteringly. The youngsters' romance has come to light, perhaps through Yvette's own admission. She may even have begged her father to help Paul. The pugnacious police chief is as furious as Bruno predicted—almost to the point of insanity, by the sound of him. And the unfortunate Madame Dompnier is caught in the crossfire.

Max props his bicycle against the hedge, opens the gate, steps into the garden and goes to the glazed doors at the rear of the villa, one of which is open. Dompnier sees him approaching. His ranting ceases. He crosses the room and draws the door almost closed, leaving it open only a hand's width through which to deal with Max.

Behind him, Yvette, still weeping, rushes from the room, followed by her mother.

Dompnier keeps hold of the door as he glares at Max. His face is flushed with rage.

"Clear off, Max. You're trespassing."

"A friendly mayoral visit, Jacques. You all sound a little upset. Is everything all right?"

"Not your concern."

"It could be, if the situation gets out of control."

"I'll decide that."

"I wouldn't want you to do anything you might regret. You wouldn't want that, either."

"Anything like what? Like giving those two a good smacking?" The two female members of his family are still audible. "Strikes me that's just what they need."

"That wouldn't be a good idea, Jacques."

The police chief seems to be calming down. He examines his scrawny fist. The knuckles are bruised and beginning to swell. He has smacked something already.

"It doesn't matter," he rasps. He raises his chin and flashes a sickly grin. "The problem will be gone soon. Midnight tomorrow—gone. Then it'll be your turn, Max."

He snorts loudly to clear his sinuses, opens the door a little further, and delivers a gob of spit that just misses Max's boot. The door slams shut. Dompnier turns his back and walks away, leaving Max gazing into a deserted room.

There is nothing more Max can do. He has issued a warning, an informal one, and that is the limit of his authority as mayor. Dompnier has committed no crime. From what Max could see, Yvette and her mother are both physically unharmed. So far anyway.

He returns to the lane, mounts his bicycle, and continues on his way.

CHAPTER 37

AT THE PICARDIE he finds that news of the morning's arrests and of Wolff's decree has preceded him.

"Monsieur Max!" sobs Virginie. "So many of you to die! Even our own Paul."

Max does what he can to calm her, then sends her home.

He goes to the kitchen.

"Auguste will be here soon," he tells Bruno.

The chef seems only half interested. "We can't let Wolff execute innocent people. You know that, Max. We must stop him."

"How do you suggest we do that?"

Bruno stares at him in surprise. "You know that too. It couldn't be simpler, we hand over our unwanted guest, your young friend—"

"Stop calling her that."

"We say we found her hiding in the grounds."

"Bad idea, Bruno. Think how much she knows about the Picardie—the escape line, the airmen. Wolff would get all of it out of her, it would be the end of the cell."

"It's the end of it anyway, without you and the others."

"Not if you're willing to take it on."

"Me? On my own?"

"There'd be our radio operator."

"But no doctor, no pharmacist, no one who can do what Auguste does, idiot that he is."

"Some of our work would have to be handled elsewhere in the line. But the cell would still operate, that's what matters, it wouldn't have to be built up again from scratch. So will you do it? Will you take over from me?"

Bruno scratches his moustache. He sighs. "If that's what you want. But I can't believe we're talking in these terms."

"We always knew the risks."

"Yes, but risks arising from the escape line itself. Not this. Your young friend has a lot to answer for." He ignores Max's glare. "So has Auguste."

"You've checked on Sophie today?"

This provokes a scowl. "Don't trouble yourself about her. She's fine. I saw what she did to the window. I tell you—we need to get rid of her, Max, it's the only way."

"Does she know about the arrests or Wolff's plan?"

"I don't see how she could. Get rid of her, Max. You're not answering me."

"How are the airmen?"

"No problems there, either."

Max takes a deep breath.

No problems.

If only.

*   *   *

Everything must be done properly, exactly as it has always been done, as if nothing has changed. Max is surprised at how calm this makes him feel.

They bring the airmen up from Duc Henri's dungeon one at a time. Max does the fetching, delivering the men to the same rear hallway by which they entered the Picardie. Bruno, in normal clothing rather than his chef's whites, which would be too distinctive and memorable, stands guard over them, armed with a pistol.

As well as following the usual procedure with the blindfold, Max wears the cap he wore last night; Bruno wears a broad-brimmed fedora. They remain behind the airmen and out of their sight as much as possible, making the men stand facing a blank wall in the hallway.

Auguste arrives. Max meets him in the courtyard.

"Recognize the bicycle, Max?"

Auguste leans the machine against a wall rather than bothering to conceal it in the barn as he would normally do.

"No need to hide it, since our Feldkommandant is no longer resident here," he explains. "Or so I hear."

"You're well informed."

"Old newshound's habits again."

Auguste knows the form and has come prepared—he has brought a battered old hat which he now tugs into place low on his head. The airmen will see little of his features, obscured by the hat and his camera.

Each airman faces the camera when instructed, with the blank wall as background. They are dressed as ordinary workers, laborers, in nondescript shabby clothing provided by the escape line. Their hair has been clipped short, hacked clumsily in order to lose the neat military cut. This too was done somewhere up the line.

Max and Bruno stand to one side as Auguste does his work. The camera whirs as he advances the film, the shutter clicks, the flash bulbs pop. It takes only a few minutes. Afterwards he and Max go outside while Bruno remains with the airmen. The chef has not spoken to Auguste; he has not even acknowledged him with so much as a glance.

"I deduce you've told him about my little indiscretion," Auguste sighs to Max.

"He'll get over it."

"I'll try to make up for it."

"What do you mean by that?"

Auguste shakes his head and instead of answering concentrates on extracting the exposed roll of film from the camera. He removes the saddle from his bicycle, slips the roll inside the frame and puts the saddle back in place.

"I still have plenty of identity card blanks," he tells Max. His voice is steady. "You'll have the finished cards tomorrow. They'll look old and well used. They'll be my usual works of art. Nothing but the best."

"Until tomorrow, then," says Max.

Auguste rubs at an eye.

"A chill in the air," he explains, and cycles off.

*   *   *

Max returns the airmen to the dungeon. As he pushes Henri's door back in place he is aware that Bruno has come through to the lobby and is watching him.

"You should go home now, Bruno. No need to stay."

"I know that."

But the chef shows no inclination to leave. He stands by the great fireplace and begins rolling a cigarette.

"You're making a mistake, Max. Do as I say and put an end to this. We can arrange things so that we don't have to worry about

how much Sophie knows and what she can tell Wolff. We can eliminate that risk entirely. Nothing easier."

"If you say so." Max knows perfectly well what Bruno has in
mind.

"Of course, I say so. All we have to do is shoot her."

The words hang in the silence that now encloses them.

A single life. That is all it will take.

*"Would you do that, Max? Would you sacrifice that life? Could you
do that?"*

Bruno concentrates on his cigarette, studying its glowing tip,
letting his proposal take shape in the curls of smoke.

It is Max who breaks the silence. "That's all? We just shoot her?
Just like that?"

"You won't have to do it. I'll take care of it."

"You'd do that?"

"For the sake of the escape line and to save who knows how many
innocent lives? I'd do it without a second thought. Wars have casu-
alties. She'll be just one casualty. She knew what she was getting
herself into when she came here. The innocent people who'll die
because of her haven't been given that choice—including young
Paul Burnand. So you tell me why not, Max."

"Well, one good reason would be because we're on the same side,
with the same enemy and the same objective. Wouldn't the
Germans love it if all they have to do is sit back while we destroy
each other?"

Bruno has taken to pacing the width of the lobby, one side to the
other and back again. At these words he breaks step and faces Max.

"On the same side? Stop dreaming, Max. You want to protect
Sophie, I understand that. I know something happened between
the two of you—I don't care what, that's not my business—but you
can't let it blind you. Would her comrades protect you and me? Do

they care about our work, about the escape line? Do they care about our innocent fellow citizens? These people are on their own side, no other. And she's on their side, no other."

"If we shoot her, how would we be any different from the Germans? How would we be different from Wolff with these executions?"

"She's no innocent, that's the difference." Bruno inhales a deep breath, releases it. "Max, you know I could deal with this myself, don't you? Without your say-so. One bullet, one corpse delivered to Wolff—problem fixed. You know I could go behind your back."

"But you won't."

"Don't be too sure."

Bruno resumes his pacing. Max watches him for a minute before speaking again.

"What if there's another way out of this?"

Bruno grunts sceptically. "What other way? What are you suggesting?"

"There's another way to prevent the executions, to give Wolff what he wants, what he needs—so that he can give High Command what it wants. There's a way to save those innocent lives. To keep the cell and the escape line safe. There's another way, Bruno. A way that would work."

"Who says?"

"Egon Wolff."

Bruno emits a sharp bark of unbelieving laughter. He wheels around and looks at Max as though he has suddenly discovered himself to be in the company of a madman.

"Egon Wolff?"

"That's what I said."

Bruno tosses the shrunken butt of his cigarette into the great fireplace.

"My God, I think you're serious."

*　　*　　*

That night it is an unhappy Bruno who leaves the Picardie and heads home. His mood is foul.

Max goes upstairs, lowers all the blackout blinds, then does the same downstairs.

He stays away from his private quarters and Sophie. He goes through to the bar, stands behind the counter, runs his hand along its cool surface. It glows like silver. More colors flash from the mirrors and bottles than he could name. He thinks of the colors in Sophie's gray eyes.

The quiet of the empty building folds itself about him. Like the streets and shaded alleys he cycled through today, the Picardie will carry on when he is gone. It is a hard thought to bear, but perhaps there is also a comfort in it.

He goes out to the grounds at the front of the Picardie. Bats are busy overhead. He skirts the old maze and stands under the plane trees.

Their leaves are still; they have nothing to say to him.

CHAPTER 38

THESE ROOMS WERE a prison where Max oppressed her with his presence; now they are a prison because of his absence.

The day crawls along but he does not come to her. What a fool she was to believe he would. She watches the mirror's little oval reflection flit across the walls of the bedroom until the daylight dies and the room falls dark.

His absence is all the more troubling because she is certain that something is going on, something bad; and it concerns him.

Voices float to her here, wisps of words and phrases, always incomplete. There is the shrill, silly woman who beats rugs and mats in the courtyard. She seems incapable of doing her work in silence. Her lamentations drift to the glassless window like the clouds of dust from her efforts.

"Monsieur Max" is how she refers to him. Monsieur Max this, Monsieur Max that. This afternoon her beating of the rugs was punctuated by bursts of sobbing and sniffles. There was mention of someone called Paul—"young Paul" and "our Paul".

Then there is the chef, Bruno. No mistaking his bad-tempered tones. But today when she heard his growl it was edged with misery.

She is convinced there was also fear. What would strike fear in such a great ox?

The one voice she has never heard, the voice she has waited to hear—has been desperate to hear—is Max's. But there has been nothing, no footsteps in the corridor, no scrape of a key in the door. He has not returned.

So she frets and chafes, lost without him, abandoned, angry because of her helplessness.

There is more than dust in the air, something more than disconnected voices hovering in the heavy atmosphere. There is something ominous, a threat, tension before a lightning strike. There is danger here. Danger for Max.

What danger?

* * *

She dreams of the dead again, and of that other prison cell, cold and damp and frightening. A police cell in Paris.

Every day the police cross-examine her, over and over until she can hardly think straight. Always the same questions. What did she know of Gérard's plan? How did she help him? Who owned the gun? Where did it come from? How did Gérard obtain it?

She has no answers for them. She tells them the truth, that she knew nothing of her brother's plan. That she did not help him in any way. That she has no idea where the gun came from. That she would have stopped him if she had known anything of his intention.

"I would never have let him do what he did," she pleads. "Can't you see? Why can't you understand?"

She is sick with fear, and sick with the loss of Gérard.

He has shamed the police by demonstrating that they are not in control of their city. They are afraid of the Germans and they keep on and on at her. They pick over her life and Gérard's life in every detail. They tell her that her friends are being questioned. Also Gérard's friends. Also her parents' friends. They tell her these people are being seized in the night, thrown into cells, intimidated and shouted at for days on end.

She is told that Maman and Papa are somewhere in these same police cells but she is not allowed any contact with them. She knows they will be at their wits' end—not only because of Gérard's death but also because of their Jewish faith. His body remains uncleansed, unaccompanied by anyone who loves him. Unburied. They cannot sit shiva. Until he is buried his soul cannot be at rest, it will drift lost and confused between two worlds, the earthly and the spiritual.

All this bears down on her, day after day, as they question her and threaten her, always the same weary inquisitors with the same maddening questions.

And then one day, without warning, the routine changes. Someone is waiting in the room to which she is brought for another round of questioning. Not one of the usual inquisitors, this person. It is a man in uniform. But not police uniform. He is wearing German uniform. He is a German officer.

There is a medical dressing on his face.

She knows at once who he is, recognizes him. This man with his unforgiving blue eyes and Iron Cross and gleaming jackboots is not just any German officer come to check on the local police at work. She recognizes him as the man Gérard wounded, the man who shot and killed Gérard.

He does not speak, never once, asks her no questions and offers no comments to her inquisitors, only stands there, hands clasped behind his back, a back as straight as if he is standing to attention. He watches and listens as she is questioned yet again. Over and over and over.

After a time, he leaves.

But she knows she will never forget that face. That handsome, ravaged German face.

CHAPTER 39

FOR MAX IT is a day of final duties.

A final stocktake. This he does in the sleepless hours before dawn.

A final reckoning of the Picardie's business accounts. The numbers are small, the task correspondingly easy; the job is done by the time Bruno comes puffing up rue de la République.

A final handwritten invoice for Wolff's account.

A final farewell to Virginie, prompting many tearful cries of "Oh, Monsieur Max!" and much wringing of her hands.

Then there is Bruno.

His temper has not improved overnight. He does not try to hide his anger. He prowls his kitchen, avoiding Max's gaze, checking things that do not need to be checked, wiping surfaces that need no wiping.

"Sit down, Bruno. You're making me dizzy."

The chef grunts. He sits down and lights a cigarette.

"The Picardie is to be yours, Bruno."

A cloud of cigarette smoke. "What?"

"After Geneviève's death, I amended my will. It's with the notary. On my death the Picardie passes solely to you. You know as much about running it as I do. It's right that you should have it."

"Max, I can't—"

"Do the best you can to keep the place going. Maybe one day it'll provide a decent livelihood again."

He passes the account books and stock records to Bruno, then presses on, leaving him no opportunity to argue.

"We'll attempt the handover of the airmen tonight. Wolff's attention will be elsewhere."

"That's one way of putting it."

"Obviously Juliette won't be able to do it. You'll have to handle it."

"So we come to it, Max. You won't change your mind?"

Max shakes his head.

"I don't agree with what you're doing. You know I don't. I can't and I never will."

"I know."

Max takes him through the how and when and where of what must happen, all of these details different from the usual procedures. Despite his anger, Bruno pays close attention.

"There's one other matter," Max concludes.

"What?"

"Sophie."

Bruno scowls but continues listening.

*   *   *

A final visit to Juliette.

"It can be done," she reports. "I was very specific about the timing and location, and they understand. The guides who'll come are the most experienced, and they'll bring no other escapers or evaders with them. Their only charges will be the ones we pass over to them."

Max turns to look at her cabinets with their bottles and jars.

"I have a further request, Juliette. It concerns your magic potions."

She regards him warily, remembering her previous clumsiness.

"Don't take anything tonight," he tells her. "Stay away from your potions."

She is dismayed. "But, Max, I'm sure to weaken—"

"You must do as I say, Juliette, you must not take anything. You'll be safe."

"How can I possibly be safe?"

"You will be. Trust me."

Her frown deepens. Then she takes a deep breath as if to steady herself, and nods her agreement.

* * *

Auguste is as good as his word. The three identity cards are not only ready; they are perfect.

He sighs as he hands them over, a ragged, uneven sound, as though it might easily have been a sob instead.

"My final job for the escape line."

"You'll be a hero to Marie."

"Yes, I intend to be."

They embrace, and Max departs.

* * *

The little Chinese mannequin has nothing to say for itself today, no messages to signal to Max or the world. On this occasion its expression is unreadable, from any perspective.

Pierre has not yet set out on his morning calls. The patients in his waiting room acknowledge Max with murmurs and glances, some of them tearful on seeing him. He is shown to a separate small room, and a few minutes later Pierre joins him.

"You're busy, Pierre. Even today, even at this early hour."

The doctor shrugs. "People still have their aches and pains. And broken bones. Yvette Dompnier, for instance."

Max looks at him questioningly.

"She broke her arm this morning. I had to set it."

"How did she break it?"

"Tripped on a stool and landed badly, she says."

Max feels his anger rising. "The same way Madame Dompnier falls down stairs? And you believed her?"

"I repair and cure as best I can, Max. That's all I can do. I don't cross-examine my patients."

"I know, and I apologize," says Max, ashamed to have chastised the old man.

He moves on to the practicalities that have brought him here.

"Bruno has agreed to take over from me. He can be ruthless, but that's good. He'll make a good leader. Better than me, I think."

The doctor purses his lips. "Anyone can be ruthless. The test is knowing when to be merciful. You've always been able to do that. We must hope Bruno can follow that path."

They regard one another in silence. Their business is done. Max can leave now and the doctor can return to his patients.

But neither of them moves.

Max looks at this man who diagnosed Geneviève's illness long before the fancy specialists in Amiens; the man who advised him when her final days were drawing near.

He steps forward and puts his arms about the doctor. And is astonished that this frail old man can still make him feel safe and protected. Even with what lies ahead.

*   *   *

Though it was not his plan to do so—not until he heard about Yvette Dompnier—he goes to the gendarmerie. He is received with cold indifference. No, the police chief is not here. No, there is no one who knows where he is, what he is doing, or when he will return: it is not for his men to question their chief's activities. But yes, they can take a message to inform him that Monsieur le Maire wishes to see him urgently.

Max departs, perfectly well aware that the message will not be passed on or, if it is, it will be ignored by Dompnier.

CHAPTER 40

THROUGHOUT THE MORNING and early afternoon there is a steady stream of callers at the Kommandantur, all hoping to persuade Wolff to reconsider, braving his wrath and for some the risk that he might add their names to his next death list.

Hortense provides Max with a commentary, knowing that all of the callers will want to look in on him as well. First to arrive are the employers and foremen of those arrested, then local teachers and school principals, then Père Bastien. They crowd the entrance hall shared with the mairie, and afterwards pack themselves into Max's office.

There is more than this local traffic. From other townships and communes come representatives of their businesses and farming associations, along with mayoral officers and leading citizens who know they are potential notables should that idea catch on, all of them anxious to prevent this worrying precedent. Even the Préfecture in Amiens sends a delegation.

Max and Hortense are soon worn out by all of them.

All these individuals and groups converge on the little railway station at Rue, which has never seen so much activity before. From there they hurry on foot or by bicycle along the dusty road to Dinon, clogging Wolff's roadblocks and testing the patience of his troopers, pushing them and their snarling dogs dangerously near to breaking point.

* * *

In the late afternoon a long black Citroën sedan draws up outside the Kommandantur and mairie.

"Well, well, look who it is," says Hortense drily. Max goes to the window.

The driver emerges and opens the rear door for his elderly passenger, a round-faced individual who climbs out slowly, stiff from the journey. He is dressed uncomfortably for the heat of the day—a cassock piped and lined in purple, a purple scarf about his waist, an unyielding white clerical collar at his throat. As he reaches up to grasp the door for support, the sunlight flashes on his gold ring with its purple amethyst. On his chest rests a large cross. As he straightens up, he positions a purple skullcap on his head.

This is Lucien-Louis-Claude Martin, Bishop of Amiens, in whose diocese Dinon is situated. With an effort he steadies himself and steps uncertainly forward. To the Kommandantur.

"To the den of the beast," says Hortense.

"He won't call here," says Max.

"Still not seeing eye to eye, you two?"

Max knows no answer is needed.

His prediction is right. Monsignor Martin leaves Dinon without darkening his doorway.

* * *

The day passes. The sun burns in a cloudless sky. Heat rises in visible waves from the cobbles of place de la Mairie. A strange hush holds

Dinon. The town's children are nowhere to be seen or heard. The day is defined by one thing alone: the midnight to which it will lead.

Max revisits the gendarmerie twice, on each occasion without success. There is still no word of Jacques Dompnier.

In the Kommandantur, Egon Wolff receives all his callers, every one. He listens to them all, every one.

And disregards them all, every one.

CHAPTER 41

HORTENSE TIDIES MAX'S desk for what they both know is the last time.

"No tears, please, Hortense."

"I wasn't offering any, Max. It's been many years since I cried over you."

But there is a prolonged embrace as she departs.

In the square outside, a German personnel carrier is cruising slowly past. A trooper is standing upright on the passenger side, repeating the same announcement over and over again through a megaphone.

"Achtung! Achtung! On behalf of the German Reich, this is an important announcement to the citizens of Dinon-sur-Authie by the Militärverwaltung in Frankreich, the Military Administration in France. Any person breaking curfew tonight, whether a citizen of Dinon or elsewhere, risks being shot without prior warning. All night-time passes for tonight are canceled. The only exceptions are the four citizens required to present themselves for arrest. Achtung! Achtung! On behalf of the German Reich . . ."

The same announcement is echoing through other streets and squares as German vehicles cruise through the town.

Max closes the door. He spends a few minutes in thought. No, he has not changed his mind. Yes, it is the right decision; there can be no other. He sought a different perspective and has found it: the only one possible. And now it is time for him to set everything in motion.

He crosses the hall to the Kommandantur, strides through the outer office, disregarding the objections of Wolff's clerical staff, and flings open the Feldkommandant's door. Wolff is at his desk. He sits back in surprise.

"Monsieur le Maire. Can I help you?"

"I've come to help you, Major."

"Indeed? How so?"

"I can give you the assassin."

A rasping voice cuts in before Wolff can reply.

"How will you do that, Max? The assassin is already in custody. Paul Burnand has confessed to the crime."

Jacques Dompnier sidles forward to bring himself into view from the corner behind the door. He looks pleased with himself, his chin thrust forward as if to carve through all obstacles.

So now his whereabouts today are explained. He has been in the German barracks where the condemned men are being interrogated. Paul's so-called confession has been beaten from him, more than likely by Dompnier himself.

"You've got it wrong, Jacques. Paul Burnand is my employee and he's no troublemaker."

"Employee? That's a little grand, don't you think? He's a kitchen skivvy. An uneducated hooligan."

"He's an honest worker with no stain on his character. He's as innocent as your own daughter. And you know it."

Dompnier blinks at the mention of Yvette. Max allows him no chance to speak.

"Have you told the Feldkommandant about Paul's relationship with your daughter? A relationship you detest. Have you told him about the rows in your family over it? The one I witnessed won't have been the only one. But they're not really family rows, are they? They're your rows. Have you told the Feldkommandant how you threatened to use violence on your wife and daughter? It wouldn't be the first time you've beaten your wife. A good smacking, you told me they needed. And now your daughter has a broken arm—how did it come to be broken, Jacques?"

"This is all irrelevant—"

It is obvious that Dompnier would carry on arguing, but Wolff has heard all he wants to hear.

"We are finished here, Monsieur Dompnier. You may leave."

"But, Major—"

"You may leave."

The look that Dompnier casts Max is one of pure hatred. The look he sends Wolff's way is no better. For a moment Max wonders if the police chief might actually unholster his service revolver and dispose of both of them.

The door of the outer office slams shut, confirming his departure.

Wolff turns to Max.

"So now you have my undivided attention, Monsieur Duval. Time is running out. I advise you not to waste it, as Monsieur Dompnier has done. You say you can give me the assassin?"

"I will personally hand him over to you."

Not a flicker of emotion passes over the scarred face. "You see? I always knew you could resolve this."

"There are certain conditions."

"Ah, conditions. You think you are in a position to impose conditions?"

Wolff studies him for a time, then waves him to a chair and summons one of the clerks from the outer office.

"Find the stenographer and bring him here at once."

He continues watching Max, an appraising glance, while still addressing the clerk.

"No armed guard will be necessary."

Afterwards Max returns to the mairie and locks up.

Leaving one final duty. The hardest of all.

CHAPTER 42

DUSK IS FALLING by the time he reaches the Picardie. He goes first to the bar, where he collects the Browning pistol and other items. As he passes the corridor to the kitchen he hears the familiar sounds of Bruno at work, rattling pans and crockery. Such normal, everyday sounds.

As soon as Max enters the bedroom she launches into a barrage of questions, marching back and forth in her bare feet as she unburdens herself of them.

"What's happened, Max? Something's happened, I know it, something's wrong. For a start, what's become of your Germans? They didn't stay here last night. One of them collected luggage trunks and kitbags and took them away. I saw him in the courtyard. Why did he do that? Are they moving out?"

He has no intention of telling her anything of Wolff's plan.

"Nothing's wrong," he says. He ignores the other questions, but she will not be appeased.

"Your Feldkommandant—where is he?"

"It's as you said—he moved out."

"Where to?"

Her interest puzzles him. She has always shown lofty indifference to Wolff and his activities. Perhaps she has finally grasped the threat he represents—not only to herself but also to the escape line.

"He and his aide have moved to the barracks."

She seems troubled by his answer but turns to other concerns.

"Your chef and that strange woman who works here, they're frightened. Are you in trouble, Max? What trouble is it? And you didn't come back to me yesterday. I knew you wouldn't, I said you wouldn't. You promised, but I should never have listened to you."

She seems close to tears. He has never seen her like this before. But what can he do? He wants to tell her that everything will be fine. That every morning the blackbird will sing, that there are dawns beyond number yet to come. He would tell her all the lies in the world if he could. All the beautiful lies. And tell himself the same lies.

"I couldn't come," he says. "It's because of the escape line. The men you saw arriving here will leave tonight. You'll be going with them."

This puts an end to her marching. Now she looks even more distressed.

"I'm leaving? Tonight?"

"You're getting out of here. It's what you've always wanted."

"But why are you sending me on the escape line?"

"It's the safest way. And I have a warning for you. I told you I suspected that your organization in Paris might not be secure. Now I know for sure it's been compromised. There's a traitor. Someone is passing information to the Germans."

"How could you possibly know that?"

"Because the Feldkommandant knows that the missing assassin isn't a citizen of Dinon. He knows you were sent here—and he knows you're still here, in hiding somewhere. This is information he didn't have a day ago. It points to an informer in Paris, someone who's reporting that you haven't returned from your mission, you and Jean-Luc. The intelligence is piecemeal—there's no mention of you being a woman—but your organization is definitely penetrated."

"If this is true, I have to warn my comrades."

"I'd advise against that. Any one of them could be the traitor, including your leaders. You can't trust anyone. You could be walking into a trap. You must stay away from your safe houses and meeting places. Make no attempt to contact any of your comrades. You'll be on your own as never before. In fact, it would be better if you didn't go back to Paris at all. Go somewhere else."

"There is nowhere else for me. You belong in Dinon, I belong in Paris."

She is right, of course. He produces the Browning and places it on the bed along with a full magazine.

"As you discovered, your pistol is no use. This one won't let you down."

He sets out her identity card, the jackknife and cash. He has brought additional cash of his own, and adds it to her small store of notes.

She watches what he is doing, but he can tell her mind is busy with other thoughts.

"Max, will you come for me when it's time? Will I see you again before I leave?"

"No. Someone else will fetch you."

"Who will that be?"

"Bruno."

"He loathes me."

"He loathes most people. But you can trust him."

"This trouble you're in—is it so close upon you that you can't be the one to fetch me, you can't even do that?"

"I'm not in trouble. It's simply that I have to be somewhere else tonight, that's all. I have no choice."

She appears to be looking at the items on the bed but her curtain of hair hides her face from him.

"Then this is farewell, Max."

"Yes, it is."

She takes a breath, releases it and pushes the hair aside. She raises her gaze to meet his. The gray eyes are solemn, their ocean as profound as ever. What he would give to surrender himself to its depths tonight.

"Max, do you think things could have been different for us? In another life, maybe?"

He is completely unprepared for that. How does he answer such a question? What can he say to this half-wild creature who has come without warning, without invitation, into his life, sowing confusion? Half wild yet so vulnerable.

It is in her vulnerability that he finds his answer. She should have hope. She is young, and the young are entitled to hope.

Besides, hope is all he has to offer. What he will do tonight he will be doing for her.

"Go from here and live your life, Sophie. Yes, I think things could have been different for us. In some other life. In another time and place."

A beautiful lie or the truth? He cannot tell. He wonders if she can.

CHAPTER 43

HE WASHES AND dresses in fresh clothing. He chooses the black suit. Black for mourning.

A restrained word of farewell to Bruno, who looks as miserable as he did that morning, then he goes through to the bar, unlocks the drawer beneath the counter, takes out Sophie's unreliable Beretta and slips it into his waistband.

He presses both hands on the counter, closing his eyes as his skin meets the cool solidity of the metal, and shuts his mind to everything but that sensation, taking it into himself as a person might take reassurance from a favored and trusted talisman. A final reassurance.

He is ready. He is at peace.

He withdraws his hand from the counter and walks from the bar. He does not allow himself a last look around. He does not look back.

In the lobby, Duc Henri gazes haughtily at him across the centuries. Max offers him a silent word of thanks.

As he crosses the courtyard towards the barn, to his regret the blackbird is silent, doing whatever blackbirds do by way of sleep. No melody to see him on his way.

He thinks of Sophie and wonders if she is watching from her empty window. He does not look around to find out.

But on rue de la République, he watches for Geneviève as he cycles through patches of moonlight towards Dinon. He does not find her.

* * *

His route takes him within a field or two of Père Bastien's little church. He hears from within the sound of singing, very faint and subdued—a melody to accompany him after all. Perhaps Geneviève would approve. If candles are burning in the church, they are few and their light is not enough to show in the stained-glass windows. Bastien is being careful. The church doors are closed. Those parishioners who have gathered within will be unable to leave until curfew ends, making for a long and uncomfortable vigil; it is their small sacrifice to honor those who are to be executed tonight.

He wonders whether their prayers can include him.

Beneath the scant moonlight, the countryside and Dinon town are also in blackout. He sees no lights in any homes or farms that he passes, nor in any of the town's business premises. No street lamps illuminate his route. Apart from the fragile singing in Bastien's church, a silence even deeper than during the day blankets the town. The street-by-street curfew warning has made sure that the streets and roads are empty. They are empty too of German patrols, with all roadblocks abandoned, their barriers raised, no sign of armored vehicles, no troopers on foot.

It is all as Max agreed with Wolff.

"Keep your troopers in check, Major," he told the German. "No roadblocks, no patrols. Make sure Jacques Dompnier keeps his men out of the way as well. Dompnier is a fool and so are his men. We don't want them blundering about."

"You are suggesting I should suspend security measures?"

"Major, the people I'm negotiating with are willing to give up the assassin because he and his accomplice acted without their authority. By their code that's an unforgivable offence. They'll bring him and pass him to me. But if they feel endangered, they'll vanish, taking him with them. They won't risk their lives over this. The decision is yours—do you want to capture the assassin or not?"

So, however reluctantly, Wolff agreed. The roads leading into and away from Dinon would be kept clear.

It was the best chance Max could give the escape line and its guides. The best chance for Sophie and the airmen.

* * *

But in terms of security, place de la Mairie is another matter. On arrival at the square Max sees that along two of its sides stand German trucks and armored personnel carriers, their engines shut down, the trucks' cargo bays lined with armed troopers, all of them as silent and still as statues, watchful and waiting. He has no doubt that every rifle and submachine gun is primed and ready. The same, he is sure, applies to the weapons held by the groups of soldiers stationed on foot along each stretch of pavement—also on the same two sides of the square, to give a clear field of fire if that is needed.

Despite the presence of so many men and their weaponry and vehicles, the square is completely silent. No shuffling of restless feet, no clank of metal. Max hears only the swish and bump of his cycle tires on cobbles as he crosses pavement and road.

He makes a slow circuit of the square and discerns the motionless forms of men stretched out in alleyways and beside some of the trucks. Their rifles are longer and bulkier than those of ordinary troopers, and rest on tripods—indicating that these are high-powered weapons fitted with magnifying sights. So these patient men are sharpshooters, snipers.

All the windows in the surrounding buildings are dark, as they are obliged to be; but along those same two sides of the square some windows are partly or fully open. There will be more sharpshooters behind them.

Max studies the rooftops. He detects no movement against the expanse of sky with its slowly drifting clouds and broken moonlight; but he is sure there will be marksmen on the roofs as well.

Having allowed himself to be persuaded to keep the rest of Dinon and its outlying areas clear, Egon Wolff has made certain that the German presence in place de la Mairie is overwhelming.

Precisely what Max has been counting on.

CHAPTER 44

SHE HEARS FOOTSTEPS. She holds her breath. Perhaps Max has come for her after all.

But the footsteps are too heavy to be his, and it is chef Bruno who appears, just as Max said. He is looking particularly sour and disagreeable. He is not wearing his white jacket and has donned a shapeless old fedora. He does not step into the bedroom, instead halting in the doorway. The cleaver is not hanging at his waist, but he is clutching a semi-automatic pistol in his massive fist.

"It's time," he growls. "Time for you to go. You'll be joining our three other special guests."

"Yes—Max said."

"Now listen. I'll be taking all of you outside. You'll all be together but you don't talk to these men, not a word. They can't speak French anyway. You keep that mouth of yours shut. I want no distractions for them. Is that clear?"

"Very clear."

"People are coming here at great risk to collect you—"

"The guides. I know."

"When you're with them, you'll do exactly as they say. There's not much moon, you'll be moving in darkness and over terrain you're not familiar with—hedges, ditches, wire fences that you can't see in the dark. It'll take all your concentration. Your guides are risking their lives for you and you don't make their work harder or more dangerous than it already is. Cause any difficulties and you'll be risking your companions' lives as well—and they count for a lot more than you." His gaze drills into her. "And understand this: if you do cause any trouble, the guides won't give you a second chance—because there are no second chances in what they're doing."

When has he ever said so much before? Why this sudden rush of unnecessary instructions?

Then, all at once, she understands. He is as nervous as she is. For the first time she notices how his hand is shaking. Disconcertingly it is the hand brandishing the pistol.

"Those are the rules—do you understand?"

She hesitates, then nods.

So the moment of her departure has genuinely come. As Max said, it is what she has wanted all along: to be out of this prison and never set eyes on it again or any other part of the Hôtel Picardie. It is what she has yearned for.

Then why this ache inside her, this emptiness?

She looks up at Bruno.

"I'll do exactly as you want," she says. "I'll follow all the rules. But just tell me one thing. Where is Max? Is he safe? Can you tell me that, at least?"

At once she sees the struggle within him that the question causes, and her heart sinks. He stares at the pistol in his fist, as though searching there for the answer.

"Tell me, Bruno."

"He's safe," the chef mutters. "Max is safe."

It is an unconvincing answer.

CHAPTER 45

No LIGHT IS showing at the windows of the Kommandantur. But Max knows that Wolff will be in there, waiting for him to bring what he needs, the trophy that avenue Kléber has demanded.

Pierre is entering the square a few paces away. The doctor seems composed and calm; he could be a man out to take the night air.

Max greets him, then Pierre turns to survey the array of trucks and vehicles and squads of troopers. He shakes his head slowly in amazement.

"All this for only the four of us?"

Max looks away, ashamed. His hope is that his old friend will forgive him, not only for what is to come but also for not disclosing it to him beforehand. A second opinion, a different perspective.

Now the silence in the square is broken by the echo of distant footsteps—but light footsteps, not German boots. A small figure becomes visible as it passes one of the trucks and approaches them. It is Juliette Labarthe. The click of her heels gathers pace as she makes out Max and Pierre, and hurries towards them. She and Pierre embrace, then she comes to Max. There is fear in her eyes as she looks around her, but also resolve, which he is glad to see.

"No magic potions," she whispers as their cheeks touch. "But I'm terrified, Max. What happens now?"

He hears the question but already his thoughts and attention have moved on. His gaze is on the nearest truck with its squad of troopers. The men are alert and vigilant, a dozen pairs of eyes watching the three of them. He tries to guess at angles and distances, a geometry of death. He thinks about the sharpshooters at the various levels where he knows or suspects they have placed themselves: on rooftops, within buildings, at upper floors and at ground level. They are certain to be more accurate at their task than regular troopers, but do they have as clear a line of sight and fire as the men in this truck?

He is aware that Juliette is repeating her question, is aware also of the glance that Pierre casts him, puzzled by his failure to respond. He hears Pierre answer the question for him. The doctor's voice seems thin and insubstantial, as if he and Juliette are not entirely real, as if the separate reality that Max has entered is the only version that matters.

"Wolff will place us under arrest," Pierre is saying. "I suppose we'll be taken to the garrison barracks."

The doctor looks at Max for confirmation but receives none, for now Max is thinking about the manner in which the three of them are standing here, so close together—too close together. He moves away from the others, hoping that they do not notice, then steps slightly forward of them. He keeps an eye on the troopers in the truck.

"And when we're in the barracks?" Juliette is asking. "What happens to us there? Interrogation? Torture?" She whispers the word as if voicing it aloud might make it more certain.

Pierre makes a gentle murmur of reassurance. "Don't upset yourself, Juliette, don't worry."

She faces Max. "I've put myself in your hands, Max. I hope I haven't made a bad decision."

This is another puzzle for Pierre. "In Max's hands? What do you mean?"

"Max, look at me." Juliette is even more fearful now. Her voice cracks, she speaks more quickly. "I've done what you asked. I have no way of cheating Wolff. You said I'd be safe. You said to trust you." She takes a step towards him.

"Stay where you are," he snaps.

She stops in her tracks, shocked by his tone.

It is finally too much for Pierre.

"What's going on, Max? Juliette, what are you talking about? What did Max ask of you?"

Before either of them can answer, the double doors of the mairie and the Kommandantur swing open. Wolff comes out and stands on the top step. He surveys the three of them—Juliette, now trembling visibly; Pierre, still calm, but perplexed; and Max.

Max, whose attention has been drawn away from Wolff and to a shadow that is separating itself from the darkness on the other side of the square.

Max, who is watching Geneviève as she returns his gaze.

CHAPTER 46

BRUNO TAKES SOPHIE along the corridor and through the kitchen to a locked and windowless hallway. Three men are standing amid a muddle of empty crates and boxes. So now the ghostly shadows she saw arriving in dead of night have become men of flesh and blood. They cannot conceal their surprise on seeing her but all of them remain silent, and it strikes her that silence in the presence of others has become their habitual state over whatever period of time they have been on the run and in hiding.

The chef marches her and the airmen—she has decided that is what they are—out to the courtyard at gunpoint. His nervousness is worse now that he has so many to control. He stays behind all of them on the walk to the archway, and, it seems to her, as much out of the men's sight as possible. This behavior and that shapeless old hat—she realizes he is trying to hide his identity from the men.

Now, as the five of them wait beneath the archway, she thinks about what happened when she asked the chef about Max's safety. His whole face altered, as if his jowls were sliding down around that moustache, as if a great effort of will had been holding everything in place until her question severed whatever threads of self-control he was relying on.

It was grief she was seeing: grief over Max. Yesterday it was fear for him that she heard in Bruno's voice; but tonight it is outright grief that she sees in his strained face.

Which can only mean that she must prepare her own heart for grief.

CHAPTER 47

MAX BLINKS. HE turns to glance at Wolff, then looks across the square again.

Geneviève has gone. Now there are only vehicles and soldiers over there, where she was, and anywhere else he looks. Nothing but the Germans and their paraphernalia of war.

But she *was* there. She is waiting. For that he is thankful.

"Monsieur!" calls Wolff. "It seems that one of your fellow notables is absent—Monsieur Froment. I hope this is not a cause for concern. I hope his courage has not failed him."

"Auguste Froment will be here."

Wolff descends a step. "And the assassin, Monsieur—where is he? You said you would bring him here, to place de la Mairie. So where is he?"

Max senses rather than sees Pierre and Juliette start in surprise; he knows they have turned to stare at him.

"What does he mean?" hisses Pierre. "Max, what's going on?"

Max moves a little further away from them, accordingly reducing the distance between himself and Wolff by a few more paces. The troopers in the truck do not react.

Wolff descends the final step.

Max checks on Pierre and Juliette from the corner of his eye. They have not moved, they have not come any closer to him.

This is the moment. It has to be. There will not be a better one.

He opens his jacket.

But gets no further. A howl cuts through the night, loud and piercing, an unearthly wail of despair that climbs in pitch then descends into a scream of anger. He swings around to locate the origin of the sound.

Auguste has entered the square, closely pursued by Marie. She may claim poor health but her lungs are fine—it was she who howled and now she continues to harangue her husband. She catches up with him, flings her arms about him and tries to pull him back, determined to prevent him joining Max and the others. They stumble together into the middle of the square.

Max watches in dismay. Until this moment everything was proceeding as he had planned. Now all is in disarray, spiraling out of his control. He can do nothing. Auguste and Marie have seized the attention of every person in place de la Mairie—every trooper in the trucks and on the pavements, and undoubtedly also the marksmen on roofs, in alleyways, in every darkened building.

But now Wolff's voice rings out again, loud and clear. And angry. "Enough!"

The command silences even Marie. She and Auguste stand frozen in place.

Most importantly, the command also brings every German eye to focus on Wolff. And, through simple proximity, on the man who has now closed the distance between them yet again.

Max Duval.

Perhaps all is not lost.

CHAPTER 48

THE FLICKER OF light was there, she saw it. It lasted no more than a single second, then was gone. She remembers how Max made his match light and immediately die.

She hears Bruno's sudden intake of breath and knows that he too has seen the signal. So has the tallest of the airmen, whose stance has stiffened.

Some seconds pass, perhaps ten she thinks, and the flicker of light appears again.

She hears the rustle of a matchbox and realizes that the chef is trying to open it while holding the pistol—and still shaking like a leaf. He will end up shooting himself or her or one of the airmen.

She hears the soft patter of matches falling to the ground.

"Damnation!"

She hears the scratch of a match being struck. But instead of bursting into flame it snaps and falls to the ground.

She stretches her arm across the chef's vast chest and, without a word, grasps the matchbox. He is so surprised—or perhaps so desperate—that he lets her take it.

She holds the box in front of her at arm's length, calmly strikes a match and blows it out immediately, she hopes exactly as required.

"Do it again," Bruno whispers. They have become partners in the enterprise now. "Ten seconds—"

But she has anticipated that and is already counting. She strikes and extinguishes a second match.

"One minute now," he says. "A minute, then it's done."

Again she counts silently, then strikes and extinguishes the third match.

She returns the matchbox to him.

She has not spoken throughout. She knows he is trying to look at her in the darkness, but she does not look up at him, instead concentrating on watching the night, this darkness that she knows she cannot trust.

Waiting with Bruno to see if between the two of them they have done things right—the way Max would have done them.

Waiting to see if she is on her way from here.

Whether or not that is what she truly wants.

CHAPTER 49

MAX CALLS OUT at the top of his voice.

"Major! The assassin is here!"

The effect of his words is immediate. Wolff tears his gaze from Auguste and Marie, and swivels to look at him.

Now is the moment for Max to bring out the pistol for all in the square to see. Now is the moment for him to raise the weapon and take aim at Wolff—but not too fast. For in that beat of time as his intention is understood, Wolff's men, his troopers and the marksmen, will see what he is doing, they will understand the danger to their Feldkommandant. They will open fire. Some of their bullets will fly wild and may find Pierre or Juliette, despite all Max's efforts to keep them distant from him and safe. But many more will assuredly find their intended target, the man who is aiming a pistol with lethal intent at their Feldkommandant.

Max Duval.

So many guns, so many bullets. His death will be quick and merciful. He will know nothing of it. There will be no interrogation of him, no confessing the truth or giving up the escape line, no betraying of Laure Rioche or Bruno. Pierre and Juliette and Auguste will walk away from here, free. The six other citizens, including Paul Burnand, will not face a firing squad. They will return to their families. There will be no further arrests or executions of innocent citizens.

There will be no doubt over his guilt: Max Duval, not only the attempted killer of Egon Wolff tonight but surely also therefore the assailant of two loyal troopers of the German Reich, the assassin for whom Wolff has been hunting with such determination.

Wolff's manhunt will be over. Sophie Carrière will be safe.

All this, to be obtained so easily.

A single life. That is all it will take.

His hand closes on the Beretta, its steel warmed by his body.

*   *   *

The night explodes. Searchlights mounted on the trucks blaze into life. Place de la Mairie becomes a blinding furnace of light. The roar of gunfire is deafening. Volleys of bullets shriek through the air. Clusters of light from barrel flashes burst and die on rooftops, in those dark windows, in alleyways, on the trucks.

Death comes speeding in the night.

CHAPTER 50

HER NERVES ARE at breaking point. She does not know what she and Bruno and the airmen are waiting for now. She did the business with the matches just as the chef instructed. So why is nothing happening? Did he get it wrong after all? Or did she?

There is a roar of gunfire in the distance. She jumps in alarm, as do all of them. The chef emits a loud groan. For a moment he seems to lose his balance and stumbles against her as if he might topple over and bring them both to the ground. She feels him make a mighty effort and steady himself. She hears him muttering under his breath but cannot make out any of his words.

She feels sure that the gunfire was in the direction of Dinon. It was the roar of many weapons but lasted only a few seconds, as if those weapons had a specific target and that target has been dealt with.

Terrible fears rush through her mind. They all involve Max.

Then, among Bruno's mutterings, she hears something that turns her blood cold. A single word, a name: Max's name. Only once does the chef utter it; but once is enough.

She rounds on him.

"What is it?" she demands. "Tell me, Bruno—has something happened to Max?"

He pays no attention. She pounds a fist against his chest. She might as well punch the wall of the archway. He seizes both her wrists effortlessly in his free hand and locks her in position at his side. He is staring over her head into the darkness.

She twists around in his grip and sees the dark figure that is moving soundlessly towards them. It halts some meters away, still too distant for her to make out any features or even whether it is a man or a woman.

"Go!" the chef growls. But the command is not aimed at her; he has turned to the airmen and is addressing them. He is no longer whispering; this time he is all urgency as he hurls the instruction at them.

"Go!" he repeats. "Now!"

They may not understand his words, but his meaning is plain enough this time, aided by the pistol that he pokes into the tall airman's ribs. The man sets out, uncertainly at first, then more confidently when the dark figure waves him onward. The others follow.

Now it is her turn. The chef looms over her. As the airmen step away he looks down at her. She catches the usual whiff of tobacco breath.

"And you now—go with them!"

He releases her wrists. She does not move.

"Damnation! What's keeping you? Get out of here!"

The dark figure is waiting for her, as are the airmen, themselves now shadows.

"What's happened to Max? For God's sake, Bruno, tell me."

The chef pushes her away. "Go! It's what he wanted. If you care so much about him, do what he wanted."

And now she runs. But not to join the others, not to follow them.

* * *

The darkness in the barn is almost impenetrable. A tremor runs through her but she holds her nerve, finds the bicycles and grabs one. As soon as she mounts it she realizes it is not the one that brought her here. But there is no time to choose another, and it will take her where she wants to go, that is all she cares about.

Seconds later she is on the road to Dinon, carrying with her that dreadful, shapeless fear that seems to have scraped out her insides.

Where is Max? What has become of him?

CHAPTER 51

THE COMBINED IMPACT of the gunfire and the blinding search-lights is physically and mentally debilitating. Max cannot move, as devoid of volition as Pierre's Chinese mannequin.

There were shouts, he remembers hearing German shouts—commands to open fire that were instantly drowned by the gunfire itself. But now there is complete silence, even more profound than when he arrived in the square, so profound that for a moment he wonders if his eardrums have burst.

Then sound returns as Wolff's troopers leap from their trucks; the crash of their steel-shod boots striking the cobbles echoes like a drumroll around the square. More commands are shouted. Some troopers take up defensive positions, others keep their weapons aimed at Max and Pierre and Juliette.

But for Max the very fact that he is feeling, hearing, seeing, sensing anything at all—even the fact that he is thinking—means that something is badly wrong. He is unscathed, untouched by a single bullet.

He is alive.

He should not be alive.

His hand still grips the Beretta. He has not brought it out, therefore it has not been observed by anyone. So there is no reason for the gunfire. No reason provided by him.

No, not by him. By whom, then?

He looks at Wolff and sees that the German is staring fixedly at the center of the square. Max shields his eyes against the blaze of the searchlights and follows the Feldkommandant's gaze.

Auguste and Marie have fallen and now lie motionless on the ground, head touching head, together in death. A shared pool of blackness, a pool of blood, is spreading around them. It gleams dully in the brilliant light.

There is something else on the ground, close to Auguste, just beyond the pool of blood. It is a pistol. Now Max understands. It is the weapon that incited the gunfire—gunfire that should have been concentrated on him.

He forces himself to move and goes over to Auguste and Marie. He is beyond caring whether Wolff will call out to forbid him or whether his men will open fire again.

He crouches down beside Marie. There is no pulse; her eyes are open, sightless, and already clouding.

He goes to Auguste. He is still breathing. Max cradles his friend's head. Auguste coughs. A stream of thick blood spills from his mouth. His torso is already dark with blood, drenched in it. Considering the number of bullets that have riddled him, it is a wonder his body is holding together.

Pierre arrives beside them, followed by Juliette. The doctor checks Marie, reaching the same conclusion as Max. Juliette begins to rip open Auguste's shirt to inspect the damage, but Pierre places a gentle hand on her shoulder and stops her with a solemn shake of his white head. His gaze meets Max's. His message is plain.

Auguste coughs softly again, a liquid wheeze.

"I didn't get the bastard." The words are barely audible.

"No matter, Auguste," Max tells him. "You're still a hero. Marie says so."

"Dear Max."

Auguste manages a sorrowful smile. A final breath, a sigh, rustles in his throat. His head falls back and he is still.

CHAPTER 52

SHE RETRACES THE route that brought her from Dinon to the railway line on that ill-fated night when she came here. This time the gradient is in her favor. Her enforced incarceration has provided her with rest and good food, restoring her strength. She covers the distance in a fraction of the time her outward journey took.

Tonight the road is as deserted as it was three nights ago—and just as dark, with its malevolent countryside blackness. All the more reason to get tonight's journey over with as quickly as possible. But tonight she sees changes. She passes through places where roadblocks seem to have been in place, presumably as part of the Germans' hunt for her—the Feldkommandant's hunt. There are barriers but they are raised now and there is no sign of any German troopers to man them. More than that, she sees and hears no trace of any Germans at all, anywhere, as she races on. No foot patrols, no vehicles, no boots crunching, no engines revving. It is surreal and unnerving, as if every last German has been made to disappear by a great magician.

But what she does discover is a glow of brilliant white light in the dark sky ahead of her. It hangs above the clustered rooftops of Dinon, suggesting that, despite the blackout regulations that are keeping every house and building in darkness, many searchlights are illuminating a part of the town. Wherever those searchlights are, they must be making it as bright as day. Why would the Germans disregard their own blackout in that manner?

Whatever is happening tonight, it is surely happening beneath that cone of light. And that is where she will find the explanation of the terrifying thunderclap of gunfire.

Most important of all, it might be where she will find Max.

So it is towards the white glow that she pushes herself, never daring to examine the darkness about her too closely, filled with fear but offering her thanks to Jean-Luc, if his soul can hear her, for his insistence back in Paris that she should memorize the map of Dinon that is still so clear in her mind.

CHAPTER 53

CLOUDS OF GUNSMOKE drift across place de la Mairie, coating Max's mouth and nostrils with a bitter residue. His hands are caked in Auguste's blood. Its metallic stink mingles with the smell of the smoke.

In the square all is still, a strange, tense calm after the storm. Wolff's men maintain their positions, awaiting his orders. All eyes are on the little tableau in the center of the square, of Max and Pierre and Juliette and those two tragic bodies in their pool of blood. Wolff has not budged from the steps of the Kommandantur.

In a single movement Max slips the Beretta from his waistband and slides it beneath Auguste's body.

He rises to his feet. Auguste has made his sacrifice, deliberately and consciously. It is not what Max wanted, it is not what he would ever have wanted, even if Marie had not been part of it, but now it falls to him to put the little printer's sacrifice to good use. He owes Auguste nothing less. And Marie.

He crosses the square to Wolff. The German is calm and composed, hands clasped behind his back in his customary stance. He seems entirely unfazed by what has occurred. From what Max can recall of the mayhem of gunfire, Wolff never flinched.

He acknowledges Max with a curt nod. Perhaps there is some-thing quizzical in his gaze.

"I assume Monsieur Froment is dead."

"He and his wife are both dead."

"I see you are angry, Monsieur. You have lost a fellow citizen and a friend. I felt similar anger at the murder of my troopers. But your anger is misplaced. My men tonight did no more than their duty in protecting me."

"They also killed Madame Froment. She posed no threat to any-one. My anger is justified."

"Her death is unfortunate but she put herself in harm's way. Let us not waste time debating this. We must move on." Now Wolff looks directly at Max. "I saw what you did just now, Monsieur. Skillfully done."

Max says nothing. Not skillfully enough, he is thinking.

"Monsieur Froment's action was stupid. Killing me would simply have made matters worse. But I know what you intended to do tonight and I salute your courage."

Again, Max is silent. He has no use for Wolff's plaudits. The truth is, he has failed. All that matters now is what the German will do. He is looking across the square at Pierre and Juliette, who are speaking quietly together. Juliette's head is bowed. Perhaps she is weeping; perhaps Pierre is trying to comfort her. Pierre removes his jacket and places it gently over the faces of Auguste and Marie. Max thinks about the explanations he must make to Pierre and Juliette, how he must account for his exclusion of them. If the executions go ahead, it will be a final accounting.

Wolff seems to be reading his thoughts.

"I think they knew nothing of your plan," he is saying. "I think you kept it from them because you knew they would never agree to it. We make lonely decisions, Monsieur, you and I. This is the burden of leadership. So let us now speak as leaders, in confidence. Not a formal meeting but a private conversation. No stenographer this time."

Max watches him warily. "Nothing on the record for Military High Command?"

A humorless smile made all the more ironic by the slant of the scar. "You understand. Good. I have a proposal for you. Dead men have their uses. High Command requires me to bring an assassin to justice, dead or alive. I will allow Monsieur Froment to be cast in that role. This will be acceptable to you, I think. So High Command will have what it demands. Your side of the bargain is this: you will undertake that the true assassin will never reappear in Dinon. Nor will any other killer come here, nor anyone with violent intent towards the Reich. There will be no acts of sabotage, no spate of attacks and killings—none of the dire things you once predicted. Give me your word on this as a man of honor, which I know you are, and let us have peace in Dinon."

"Major, I want that as much as you do—but I can't guarantee it. There are those who are committed to a path I would never pursue. They'll always be there; they'll always exert their influence. I'll do my best to counter them but I can't guarantee what you ask."

"You have steered Dinon away from such influences until now. I will trust you to do all in your power to do so again. That will be sufficient. Let us see how we fare."

"Why would you trust me?"

"Because of what you were prepared to do tonight."

"You'll call off the executions and release my citizens? And there'll be no other executions?"

"That is what I propose. But only if you accept your part."

Max thinks about Auguste. This is what his sacrifice has bought.

He thinks about Dinon returning to how it was before the hard men sent murder and bloodshed. He thinks about the escape line being able to resume its work.

He thinks about Sophie, even now on her way to safety.

His decision could not be clearer.

"Then we are agreed, Major."

CHAPTER 54

SHE IS NOT on her way to safety. She is crouching in an alleyway, in the doorway of what was once a boucherie, its windows plastered with German propaganda posters. The alley leads to the main square, which she remembers is called place de la Mairie. It is flooded with light, the cone of blazing white light that she followed to come here.

The Germans are there in force, making up for their absence elsewhere. Twenty or thirty troopers line the sides of the square along with trucks and personnel carriers. There may be others that she cannot see. It is a massive display of military power—and undoubtedly the origin of the gunfire. She can even smell its aftermath in the air.

She stretches forward, cautiously, so that she can see more of the square. In its center stand an elderly white-haired man and a woman whose face is hidden because her head is bowed. Two bodies lie on the ground beside them, clearly dead—presumably the victims of that terrible burst of gunfire. They are partly covered by a cloth or coat.

The sight makes her sick with fear. Is one of them Max?

She stretches forward again, as cautiously as before.

And sees Max. He is alive and unharmed. Relief floods through her. He is standing at the edge of the square, near the Kommandantur and the mairie. He seems to be talking with someone.

She stretches forward again—and draws back instantly when she sees the man who is standing beside him.

It is the German. The Feldkommandant.

CHAPTER 55

"Now some essential formalities," Wolff tells Max.

A gang of troopers approaches Pierre and Juliette, their rifles trained on them and on the bodies of Auguste and Marie, either of whom might in theory still be alive and dangerous. Pierre and Juliette are searched. No weapons are found on them. Two troopers push Max back to the center of the square at gunpoint and search him. Nothing is found. Auguste and Marie's bodies are checked for signs of life, then also searched. A trooper takes possession of Auguste's pistol. He finds the Beretta and takes it as well, showing no surprise that Auguste was apparently armed with more than one weapon.

It is time for the bodies to be taken away. Wolff summons one of his officers and speaks to him. The man clicks his heels, delivers a salute and departs.

Wolff calls to Max. "I have instructed that the bodies are to be buried in unmarked plots, as was done with the other assassin. There will be no religious ceremony."

"Major, that is a cruel—"

"Save your breath, Monsieur. Look to the living, not the dead."

He returns to the Kommandantur.

To make the telephone call that will spare those innocent lives.

CHAPTER 56

SHE HAS CIRCLED around the network of streets behind place de la Mairie, reaching the narrow lane that runs along the side of the Kommandantur and mairie. She hears voices and activity in the square. In the lane she finds several doors. In the spill of light from the square she notices that the ground outside one of the doors is littered with small white scraps of paper. They turn out to be flattened cigarette butts. She tries that door; it has been left unlocked. She enters.

In the corridor she waits for her eyes to adjust, then follows the sound of the German's voice. It leads her to what seems to be a main entrance hall at the front of the building. Off this hall on one side is an office with several desks. This in turn brings her to another office, where a light is burning. She has heard no other voice in the building, has heard no one moving about but him.

In the center of the inner office stands a meeting table surrounded by chairs. He is standing at the desk beyond the table, his back to her.

Her heart is hammering. She waits in the doorway while he speaks on the telephone. It is a one-sided exchange; he seems to be issuing a series of orders.

The call ends. He replaces the handset. Before he can turn around, she racks the slide of the Browning pistol, loading a round into the chamber.

The metallic sound is unmistakable. He freezes.

"Raise your hands."

He obeys. She steps forward, skirting the table and chairs, and tries to unfasten his holster so that she can remove the Luger pistol. But her detour around the table has put her at an awkward angle and her fingers, still stiff from the injuries sustained during her struggle with the bedroom window, fumble at the task.

It is all the opportunity he needs. His right arm swoops down, he seizes her wrist and twists it, very hard. His left hand snatches the Browning from her weakened grasp, his right elbow drives into her midriff.

She staggers back with the momentum of the blow, doubled over and winded, dazed by the pain in her wrist, which feels as if it might be broken. She collides with a chair and barely manages to recover her balance.

She is helpless. She knows it. He must know it. He can shoot her now.

Her body is turned away from him. The Browning presses against her skull. She waits for the bullet. A single thought spins around in her mind. It will be her last thought on this earth, and it leaves no room for anything else, no room for prayer, no room for regret, no room for hatred, no room even for any sense of injustice. It is the thought that this man shot Gérard and now he will shoot her. He killed the brother; now he will kill the sister.

But no bullet comes. Instead, he reaches out and whips the beret from her head—just as Max did, once. The suddenness of the act and the force of that memory make her gasp.

With the beret gone, her hair falls free, obscuring her face. The muzzle of the Browning pushes the hair aside. The German comes closer to her and she hears his intake of breath as he sees her face. The gun stays in place; her face remains fully visible as he studies her. She fixes her gaze on the floor and tries to make herself pray.

She watches his boots as he steps first to one side of her, then to the other.

At last, he breaks his silence.

"Look up. Look at me."

She raises her head, looks directly at him, sees the scar, and sees also the slight widening of his eyes as his recognition of her is confirmed. Perhaps prompted by her gaze, he lifts a hand towards his face, as though he would touch the scar, but he stops himself.

The pistol moves away from her skull, although it is still trained on her.

"I remember a very scared young woman."

He speaks slowly, like a man preoccupied—as if he may be sifting through the past as she has done so often; and as she is doing now.

"I see her again now, here, that same young woman. She is still scared, I think."

"Wrong. I'm not afraid of you."

"No? I have to ask myself why this young woman is in Dinon. Who has been sheltering her, who has been protecting her? Did she come here to murder me in an act of vengeance? Or was it to assassinate my loyal troopers? And then, after doing that, by good fortune or bad she discovered me as well. So many questions."

He pauses, thinking. She listens to his breathing.

"But in the end these questions do not matter. The outcome for this young woman must be the same, whatever the circumstances that brought her to this moment. She and I both know that. Fortunes of war."

Sounds from outside enter the room, the sounds of his troopers clattering about in the square. He glances towards the door as if conscious that he should be returning outside. But he shows no inclination to do so.

It is a while before he speaks again.

"He was your brother. I remember that too."

Sudden tears prick behind her eyelids. Tears of anger with this man as well as tears for Gérard.

These are the final seconds of her life. Why does the German delay?

He leans back against the desk. He seems lost in his thoughts. He is still gazing at her but she realizes that he is focused on an internal landscape of his own.

"Your brother. Your late brother."

She sees that he is holding the Browning only loosely. She wonders if she can muster the strength and speed to seize the weapon back from him. She wonders if her injured wrist is strong enough. Even if she fails, she will have tried—better than waiting like a beast for slaughter, better than waiting for him to pull that trigger.

But she has delayed too long and her chance is gone. He has returned from wherever his thoughts had taken him. She curses her indecisiveness. His grip on the weapon becomes firm again. He presses the muzzle into the soft flesh under her chin and raises her head so that she is looking at him again.

"Do you have another weapon? Are you still armed?"

She shakes her head. Evidently he believes her, for he makes no move to search her.

"Ammunition?"

He extends a hand. She retrieves the spare magazine from her pocket and gives it to him.

He leans back against the desk. But this time he seems to have made a decision. He releases a long breath.

"You are one assassin too many."

She has no idea what he means.

CHAPTER 57

IN PLACE DE la Mairie, Max and the others wait, held at gunpoint by Wolff's troopers. With so many German ears all around them, Max has yet to give Pierre and Juliette any explanation of his dealings tonight with Wolff. So far he has told them only that they are all to be released—not only the three of them but also the six citizens already in custody.

"We have Auguste to thank for this," he adds. "Auguste and Marie."

"God rest them," whispers Juliette.

Max knows that he will not tell Pierre and Juliette everything; there is no need for them to know his plan as it was. Only Bruno knows that, and the information will stay with him.

Long minutes have passed now since Wolff returned to the Kommandantur. Pierre is becoming restless. Juliette looks exhausted.

"What's taking so long, Max?" grumbles Pierre. "What's Wolff doing in there? It's just a telephone call."

Max is as puzzled as Pierre.

"He'll have to clear everything with High Command, I suppose. And it's the middle of the night."

The generals in avenue Kléber may be asleep, but with Teutonic efficiency the bodies of Auguste and Marie have already been taken away and now the center of the square is being hosed clean. Soon all traces of blood will be gone. Come sunrise the spot where Auguste and Marie died will be dry and clean, showing no evidence of what happened.

But Dinon will know. Dinon will not forget. Max and the others will see to that. Auguste and Marie—heroes both. Even Bruno will allow Auguste that accolade.

Max glances around the square. Pools of shadow merge as one by one the searchlights are extinguished and place de la Mairie gradually returns to darkness. All the trucks and most of the armored personnel carriers are beginning to withdraw in a haze of exhaust fumes and rumble of heavy tires on cobblestones, scattering to resume their normal night patrols.

And still no sign of Egon Wolff. Pierre grumbles and glares at the troopers guarding him and Max and Juliette.

At long last the double doors open. Wolff appears. But only to summon an officer.

"Now what's he playing at?" mutters Pierre.

Wolff returns to the Kommandantur. The officer dismisses the troopers holding Max and the others. He orders Pierre and Juliette to go home, but escorts Max to the doorway of the Kommandantur and gestures with his rifle for him to enter.

Max finds Wolff standing by his desk.

"What took so long, Major?"

"Monsieur le Maire, I have informed Military High Command that the assassin has been handed over to me as required—dead, unfortunately, so of course he is of no further interest. High Command has rescinded all the execution orders and has approved the release of your six citizens. You and the other notables are also free to go, of course. The six ordinary citizens will leave the barracks within the next hour. Provided they go directly to their homes, they will not be considered to be breaking curfew and my men will allow them to pass unhindered."

"I hope your interrogators have left them physically capable of making the journey to their homes."

Wolff ignores that.

"I have fulfilled my part of our agreement," he says. "I trust you will remain mindful of yours."

"I'll do all in my power."

Max turns to leave. But Wolff has not finished.

"A moment, Monsieur."

Wolff takes something from a drawer in the desk and turns it over in his hands. It is an old black beret. It has seen better days. The cloth is scuffed, the stitching along the leather edging is beginning to fray, there are green stains on the fabric, as if it has been dragged through undergrowth.

There must be millions of berets like it in France. In Dinon alone there may be a thousand. Who would care about this particular beret?

And how has it ended up in Egon Wolff's hands?

Max returns the German's gaze in silence. No accusation has been made, no guilt suggested, no denial required or offered.

Wolff hands the beret to him without a word.

Without a word Max accepts it.

CHAPTER 58

AT EVERY INSTANT as she cycles through the darkness, she expects to feel bullets hammering into her back. What better reason for the German to release her than to make her target practice for his troopers, a night's sport? An unarmed target at that. He told her she had only minutes in which to make her escape; soon his patrols would begin moving out of place de la Mairie to take command of the roads and streets again. But why should she trust him? He knew she had come to kill him, so why would he give her this chance? He did not explain why the patrols had been withdrawn from the roads in the first place. He refused to tell her what had happened in the square—why people had been shot or who they were. She does not know what Max's role was, or even whether he is now in custody. She asked, but the German explained nothing.

"One assassin too many."

What did that mean?

The night is so dark that she can barely see the road beneath her wheels. There is only the slimmest sliver of moon and even that is hidden by cloud. Neither moonlight nor starlight finds a way through. Now all her irrational response to the deep darkness of this countryside returns, stronger than ever. The darkness feels like a living entity that opposes her and through which she must force a path. She shudders, as much from the terrors conjured by that hostile blackness as from fear of any human adversary.

She is on a narrow lane that runs between fields of corn. On either side of her the corn rises like walls, standing higher than her head. An owl is hooting. There is no wind, but over the chirp and buzz of nocturnal insects she hears a constant rustle from the corn as she passes between the fields, as if unseen hands are shaking the stalks and leaves. She turns her head to look, every hair on her body prickling and rising even though she knows she will see nothing, for there is nothing to see.

But when she looks back at the lane the woman is there, right in front of her.

There is no time to wonder where she came from or how she got there. There is no time to think. Only to brake, as hard as possible.

The bicycle skids on loose gravel, slewing out of control to one side, taking itself and Sophie off the lane and into the corn. She crashes to the hard-packed earth among the closely planted rows, dazed and disorientated, her injured wrist racked by spasms of pain from the fall.

She manages to get to her feet. The woman has gone.

Now she hears the truck. There must be a road or lane up ahead that cuts across this lane on which she is traveling; the truck has come from that other road, the sound of its engine absorbed by the corn until it turned the corner. The vehicle is audible now as it rumbles closer.

She realizes that her bicycle is still partly in the lane and will therefore be visible. She dives forward, drags it out of sight, raises it upright and scrambles further into the corn, taking it with her and going as far and as fast into the field as she can. She prays that the movement of the stalks is not noticed as she pushes between the rows.

The truck comes alongside the place where she is hiding. A searchlight clicks into life. Its beam projects straight ahead, then sweeps from side to side, casting confusing shadows all around. But there is enough light at the margins of the beam for her to make out the figures standing in the open bed of the truck.

Contrary to her expectations, these are not the German Feldkommandant's men. These are not his troopers in their field gray. These are men in dark uniforms. They wear caps, not German helmets. They are not soldiers of any kind. They are French police. One of them, an undersized little man, snorts loudly, so loudly that she hears it above the noise of the engine. He spits over the side of the truck into the lane.

These men are her own countrymen. But that will be no help to her. The French police are as bad as the Germans. The men who arrested her and Maman and Papa after what Gérard did, they were her countrymen. So were the ones that Maman and Papa reported to at the gendarmerie when they were sent for in the roundup, the ones who took them away, never to be seen again. As she told Max, the French police do the Germans' dirty work for them.

She remains very still, close to the earth and sheltered by the corn. The truck passes by. The beam of the searchlight diminishes in the distance. The truck's engine note grows fainter. Finally there is silence.

It is broken by a voice.

"You can come out now."

She recognizes that deep growl.

"Come out," repeats Bruno. "It's safe. Dompnier and his clowns are too stupid to think about doubling back."

"Dompnier?"

"Our chief of police. That's who that was."

"He's revolting. He spits."

"He does worse than that. A good man to avoid."

She takes a few steps back towards the lane. She sees his bicycle.

"You've been following me? Why?"

"Max made you my responsibility. I was with you as far as the alleyway, then I lost you. Where did you go?"

She sees no reason to tell him. "I just steered clear of the Germans. Anyway, it seems you found me again."

"I checked the streets around place de la Mairie until you reappeared."

"So you were here, tailing me. Out here."

"Obviously."

She has reached the lane now and is standing beside him. She peers up at the heavy face. In the darkness the moustache is the only feature she can make out.

"Then you must have seen," she says. "If you were here, you must have seen."

"I saw you take a tumble, if that's what you mean. Lucky you didn't break a leg. But it got you out of Dompnier's way just in time. Another bit of luck."

"Yes, but did you see the woman?"

He looks down at her. His eyes are in deep shadow. "What woman?"

She shakes her head, abandons her questions. No point pursuing the matter. There are secrets that the darkness will always keep to itself. Finally, perhaps, she is learning.

She mounts the bicycle.

"That was hers, that bicycle," Bruno says.

Sophie hears him but she is already on her way.

She knows who the woman was. In her heart she knows. She saw the photographs and she knows.

PART THREE

LIBERATION

CHAPTER 59

1945. FRANCE HAS been liberated.

The Germans are gone now, long gone, and Dinon belongs to the Dinonnais again. It is as Max always wanted, what he was determined to secure: his beloved Dinon has survived.

As did the escape line, operating right to the end.

Four graves have been sliced neatly into the good earth of Picardy. A summer storm has burst. Rain lashes the graveyard in erratic gusts, drumming on the coffins as they are lowered. Max can see it will not be long before the rain erodes those neatly cut edges. Already there are shallow pools in the graves, their sides temporarily shored up with slats of wood, so that each coffin, its contents by no means heavy, floats and shivers briefly before coming to rest.

Père Bastien huddles with his prayer book beneath an umbrella someone is holding for him. The mourners are many; they crowd the paths winding through the graveyard and fill the lane all the way back to the little church. It seems to Max that all of Dinon must surely be here. All of Dinon and all who worked for freedom, for liberation—Bruno, Pierre, Juliette, Laure Rioche.

The bodies, little more than bones and rags after such a passage of time, had to be exhumed, retrieved from the unnamed plots to which they had originally been consigned. Now they are being reburied with the dignity they deserve. Having had this first resurrection, they can rest in peace now in anticipation of their next.

Auguste and Marie have been buried side by side. It was Max's decision that Jean-Luc should be laid to rest beside them—a fellow patriot, Auguste would say. In any case the young man had no family to claim his body, no family grave to receive him. So let Dinon be his family.

Everything is done now; all the prayers have been said. The mourners are starting to leave. It will take a good while for them to turn about and retrace their steps in the narrow paths that have become mud-churned and slippery. At least the rain has stopped. There is the subdued murmur of many conversations, something else that will slow things down.

Max is content to linger. Time for reflection. Bastien too is taking his time. He slips his prayer book into a pocket and comes over to join him.

"The old priest had his views," he tells Max. "Mine are different. It took a while to sort things out—Rome moves slowly at the best of times, and these recent years have been anything but the best of times. But now your Geneviève rests where she belongs, in consecrated ground."

Max watches as the gravediggers remove the shoring planks and the soil climbs higher in the graves. He has brought cash for the men. They will have a hearty thirst by the time their work is finished.

Sophie Carrière is here. She has come from Paris for the exhumations and reinterments. No tattered vagabond now, but dignified in black. Black for remembrance.

They have not yet spoken, she and Max, but he knows they will. No hurry. He knows there will be time. There will be dawns beyond number.

"Do you keep your promises, Max?"

"Always."

He looks up at the sky. The clouds are clearing, the sun is breaking through. Sunlight falls like a blessing on the graveyard.

Somewhere overhead a blackbird begins to sing.

AUTHOR'S NOTE

Many traces still remain in France of the Second World War and, in particular, of the French Resistance. Those who fought and died as members of the Resistance are honored in streets and village squares named for them. There are wall-mounted plaques commemorating their execution, and monuments by the side of country roads and in fields where they met their death. Many were heartbreakingly young.

Resistance could take many forms, such as sabotage, the publication and distribution of anti-Nazi leaflets, and the operation of secret escape lines that enabled stranded Allied airmen and others to escape from Nazi-occupied territory. It was a time of great courage and self-sacrifice. People had to make choices—how to survive from one day to the next; whether to resist the Nazi occupier, with all the dangers that entailed. These choices were unimaginably difficult.

I hope *Landscape of Shadows* can help us remember those who took the road of resistance in whatever form. In fighting to defeat Nazi oppression they put their lives on the line not only for France but for all of us.

DISCUSSION GUIDE
FOR BOOK CLUBS

1. What do you think of the very different ways in which Max and Sophie oppose the German occupation?

2. *Dinon is full of collaborators.* Do you think the people of Dinon are collaborators? Are there characters who clearly are not collaborators?

3. What part does the loss of loved ones play in the novel?

4. Do you think Sophie is a murderer or a freedom fighter? What factors led you to this conclusion?

5. What is the moral dilemma that Max discusses with Doctor Pierre? What is the effect on the subsequent action of the novel?

6. Egon Wolff serves an evil regime. Is he himself evil? What leads you to believe this?

7. Do you think Sophie develops in maturity or wisdom in the course of the novel? Why do you believe this?

8. How important are minor characters such as Doctor Pierre, Bruno, Auguste, and how do they influence what happens?

9. *Anyone can be ruthless. The test is knowing when to be merciful.* What examples are there of characters being merciful?

10. Do you think religious faith has a role in the novel? If yes, why? And in what way?

PUBLISHER'S NOTE

We hope that you enjoyed *Landscape of Shadows*, the second historical thriller novel by Kevin Doherty published by Oceanview. The first was the highly acclaimed, award-winning *The Leonardo Gulag*.

THE LEONARDO GULAG

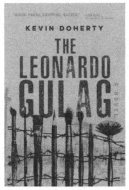

A journey into the sinister heart of Stalin's regime of terror, where paranoia reigns and no one is safe.

A brilliant young artist. A forced-labor camp in the Arctic gulag. His task: forge the drawings of Leonardo da Vinci. Only option: perfection.

"[*The Leonardo Gulag* is] vivid, fresh, gripping, clever. This historical thriller set in a gulag in Stalin's Russia thoroughly propelled me. With appearances from Stalin himself and Soviet spy Anthony Blunt, it feels authentic on every page. I felt I was there."

—DAVID MORRELL,
New York Times best-selling author

We hope that you will enjoy reading Kevin Doherty's *The Leonardo Gulag* and that you will look forward to more to come.

For more information, please visit Kevin Doherty's website: www.kevindoherty.com.

If you liked *Landscape of Shadows,* we would be very appreciative if you would consider leaving a review. As you probably already know, book reviews are important to authors and they are very grateful when a reader makes the special effort to write a review, however brief.

Happy Reading,
Oceanview Publishing